TWINS
TANGLED
and
TORN

I0460525

TINY TREE

TINY TREE

Twins Tangled and Torn
Published in 2025 by
Tiny Tree Books
West Wing Studios
Unit 166, The Mall
Luton, LU1 2TL
tinytreebooks.com

For Mum, with all my love and thanks

My heartfelt thanks to all members of my family for their unwavering love and support over the years, and for always taking an interest in my writing. I am so grateful.

I am indebted to the Tiny Tree team for all the hard work and dedication that has gone into producing this book - in particular to James Shaw for his astute design and editorial input, and for pushing wide for me that magical publishing portal, when so many had kept it firmly closed, and to Anthony Barlow for his promotional skill and expert marketing knowledge. Thanks to both for being so very pleasant and approachable throughout.

And special thanks to you, the reader.

Chapter One

There comes a moment in a teenage girl's life when she has to break away from her twin sister and get a life of her own. Not an easy thing to do when you've been stuck to your twin like super glue for the last fifteen years! At first, I was petrified. But the moment I realised this was what I had to do, was the moment my life started to change forever.

Arabella and I sleep in the same bedroom but at opposite ends, because she is a light sleeper and doesn't snore, and I am a heavy sleeper and do. Her end of the room is bright canary yellow with tiger streaks of orange paint splashed across the walls – very exotic and very her. My end is pale blue with a touch of cream around the skirting and no haphazard splashes anywhere. I'm no psychologist, but what this seems to say is that Arabella is bold, extroverted and colourful, and I am reserved, introverted and not so colourful. And these aren't the only differences between us.

Arabella is: tall, leggy, white-blonde.

I am: medium height, medium legged, brownie-blonde.

Arabella is: very good at science, hates poetry and art, and is the angel of the boys' changing rooms, and cries a lot, and wants to be a doctor when she grows up.

I am: average at science, love poetry and art, and am no-one's angel, and try not to cry or show my emotions to anyone, and have no idea what to be when I grow up.

No-one knew Mum was having twins. When Arabella was born, everyone clustered around the bed cooing. She cried a lot but stopped as soon as someone picked her up (no change there then!). Her entry into the world was like something out of a fairy tale, with everyone looking on, spellbound by her beauty. But then there was a humongous rumpus in Mum's belly and the top of my head appeared between Mum's thighs, totally flummoxing the midwife: "Blimey, there's another one coming! How did I miss that?"

Fifteen minutes later, I was on the way, a purple, writhing blob on Arabella's beautiful landscape. Nobody cooed or drooled over me, or showed any emotion, except shock horror. I remember, you see; not in the way you remember facts but in a hazy, atmospheric kind of way: the hard, staring eyes, the eerie silence of the hospital room, broken only by my wails, the cold, cold feeling of not being expected.

Sounds grim, doesn't it? Actually, it picked up after that. Even though I wasn't expected, Mum *did* want me, and so did Dad, and Arabella and I, for better or worse, became very close.

Here's an example of why it's time to break away from Arabella and get a life of my own. It's a blustery night in March: eight p.m. to be exact. Mum is downstairs paying bills on the internet, I am in our bedroom, doing my homework with the door ajar (because I hate the lonely feeling I get when the door is closed tight). Arabella is lounging in a steam-filled bath of peach-scented bubbles, listening to Radio One. She's finished her homework (fifteen minutes before me, just like the interval between our births). Bruno, our mum's live-in boyfriend, is making hot chocolate in the kitchen.

Bruno comes upstairs, hands me a mug of hot chocolate and shouts to Arabella that hers is outside the bathroom door. There's no sound from inside the bathroom, other than the odd blast of pop music. Perhaps Arabella has fallen asleep in there. Bruno gets worried and calls to her again. Finally, Arabella's little tinkle of a voice pipes up.

"You mean with marshmallows and cream, Bruno?"

"No, with plain milk."

"But you always make it for me with marshmallows and cream. It's the *only* way to have it!"

Now, there aren't many things the male sex won't do for Arabella, but on this occasion Bruno refuses to grant her request.

"I can't go down again. I'm tired and I've work to do upstairs. If you want it with marshmallows and cream, you can get out of the bath and make it yourself!"

"But I've only just got in," she squeaks, slithering around and making a loud whooshing sound with the bath water, so Bruno can hear. "If I get out now, it'll be a total waste of water and a total waste of Mum's electricity. Please, it'll only take a few minutes. No-one makes hot chocolate like you do, Bruno. The cream's always hand whipped to perfection," (*funny that, I think, when it comes straight out of a can*), "and you do this awesome thing with the marshmallows, where a trail of them hits your mouth instead of just one or two. Tops Costa any day!"

All this flattery suddenly means Bruno doesn't know what to do. He picks up the mug of hot chocolate, puts it down, picks it up again, puts it down, picks it up, sees me staring at him. Now, Bruno's a pasty-faced guy, but right now I could toast muffins on him. He smiles an embarrassed smile, nods like I'm some sort of acquaintance and shoots downstairs, only to return three minutes later with an oversized mug of hot chocolate, brimming with cream and marshmallows. He gives a quick tap on the bathroom door, shouts to Arabella it's outside and scuttles off to his computer room, and I don't see him again all evening.

Once Arabella's out of the bath, I quiz her about it.

"What was all that with you and Bruno earlier?"

"All what?" she says, like butter wouldn't melt.

"You know, ordering him around and getting him to run up and downstairs for you, like he's some kind of waiter. I think Mum should know. I think I should…"

Arabella clamps my mouth with her bath-moistened hand and pins me to the bedroom wall.

"Upset Mum and I'll upset *you*!" she cries. "You're just jealous because you can't get anyone to do anything for you, and you don't look like this!"

She whips off her towel and stands starkers in front of me. Her skin is all pink and plump from the hot bath, her legs soft and shiny as satin, her breasts like cupped mushrooms.

I feel sick and faint and frightened all in one go. I look down at the mustard zigzag of our bedroom carpet, thinking any second there could be a few more zigzags there. Then I rush out of the bedroom, up to the loft and stay there, safe in the privacy of my own company.

There are a few things I need to learn from this incident, which, late at night, tossing and turning in bed, I attempt to take on board:

1. I *am* a touch jealous of Arabella – but only a *touch*, and there's stuff about her I'm not jealous of *at all*.
2. I need to stay out of her business, otherwise it could get me and other people into hot water.
3. Arabella is always using me and putting me in compromising situations, where I am sworn to secrecy *or else*! She'd say that's what twins are for. I say I'm tired of it. *Right now, Arabella is very bad for my self-esteem, and I have to make the break.*

The psychotherapist, Jung, would have had some very interesting things to say about my relationship with my twin. He was Swiss, practising around nineteen hundred, and believed that in every girl there's a male side called the animus, and in every boy a female side called the anima.

At its worst, when left to do what it likes, the animus can make girls quarrelsome and opinionated, and the anima can make boys overemotional and wimpy. But, at best, the animus and anima show how a girl isn't just frilly dresses and make-up and baking cakes and making babies but has masculine urges too, like wanting to kick a ball or reason out a problem instead of bursting into tears over it, and that a boy, whether he'll admit it or not, has girlie bits that make him want to be a hairdresser rather than a rugby player or cry when he's hurt. I learnt more in Mrs Field's lesson on Jung than I've learnt in all my years at school, because Jung introduced me to the different sides of myself.

It is Tuesday, a sunny day in April, and two full weeks since I made the pact with myself to be more independent of Arabella. So far, I haven't quite managed to make the break, so I'm still her lapdog and still letting myself be forced into the role of third wheel with her and her endless boyfriends. I ask you, who in their right mind would want their twin sister hanging around while they kiss and cuddle their latest conquest behind the telegraph pole? No-one! But Arabella does and, like a fool, I go.

I like Shaun. He's the only one of Arabella's boyfriends I have liked and believe me there've been bucketfuls! He's not rough or spiteful or rude to me. When I pop my head round the telegraph pole, he doesn't say "What the *fuck* are you doing here? Get lost, will you!" He's too kind and gentle for that. I don't mean he wouldn't prefer it if I *weren't* around, but circumstances being what they are, he puts up with me.

The worst thing Shaun has ever done to me is ignore me, and if I had to choose, I'd rather be ignored than told to *fuck* off. Shaun plays the saxophone in the same orchestra that I play the violin. We make music together, and *boy*, do we do it well! At first, Shaun didn't speak to me – not for weeks of rehearsals. Then he latched on to me being Arabella's twin (this was before they were going out) and paid me loads of attention. His reasons were a bit obvious – ignoring me one minute, falling over me the next – but at least he was polite. Sometimes, though, he was so cringingly polite and nice, the rest of the orchestra got the wrong end of the stick, and I had to explain, "No, it's not me he fancies. It's my twin."

My admiration for Shaun extends beyond his polite, cordial manner. He plays the saxophone exquisitely, like a budding John Coltrane, gently taking possession of the instrument with his mouth, like he's seducing it. The sound he produces is *incredible*: high and low, soft and hard, light and deep, all at the same time. Miss Corder's so impressed she's thinking of entering him for *Young Musician of the Year*.

But all this praise doesn't mean I admire the way Shaun takes possession of Arabella, like he's gobbling her up. The sucking sounds they make are disgusting and as far from the melodious sounds of the sax as you can get. All yucky, mucky slurping, blowing, sucking and clucking with their lips. On my second excursion with them, round the back of the wheelie bins in the council car park, I make sure I take some ear plugs and stand with my back to them, so I can't hear or see a thing. The only time I glance round because I *have* to – otherwise an oversized pigeon will dollop on Arabella's head and she'll *never, ever* forgive me – Shaun has his hand up Arabella's skirt and is fingering her thigh, and other bits too. I can't believe my eyes, nearly forget the pigeon and its poo, and only just yank Arabella out of the way in time.

"Urrrrrr!" Arabella shrieks, as the streaky white dollop splatters next to her big toe.

She lightens up when she realises it hasn't landed ON her, pulls down her skirt and announces it's time to go. But Shaun isn't ready to go; he's been enjoying himself too much.

"What, go now?" he stammers, like he can hardly believe his ears.

"Yes, come on Babes, I need to catch up on *Hollyoaks*."

"Babes", by the way, is me, not Shaun. Odd, isn't it? Logically, it should be Shaun, he being Arabella's boyfriend and the pet or affectionate name girls often give their boyfriends. But no, Babes is me, fully and squarely, because to address me with such a name is the only way Arabella can reconcile herself to using me as her nursemaid or mother figure in the scenario. Psychologists would call it something like displacement of roles. Arabella wants me to provide her with all the support and nurture of a mother, but she can hardly call me Mummy because that would put me in a dominant role and there's no way she's prepared to give away her power to me *that much*. So, it's Babes instead, thereby securing from me what she wants while keeping me in a submissive role. Clever, isn't it? Or maybe I'm the clever one. Maybe I've just come up with a new and totally original theory for twin rivalry. Perhaps my inner power is growing faster than I know.

Arry – sometimes I call her this – and I trundle in one direction, and Shaun trundles in another, looking thoroughly doleful.

The third time I accompany them, it's to see a classic – Pitch Perfect – a film I actually want to see. I like to think Arabella has taken my choice of film into account, but chances are she wants to see it even more than me. We sit in the back row, along with all the other fondling couples and, being the only gooseberry, I feel very left out. Arabella plonks herself between Shaun and me and controls the king-size box of popcorn she's bought with her own money, every few minutes handing a fistful to me and a fistful to Shaun and scoffing the rest herself. I know then I should have bought my own box, but didn't because in theory a king-size box is more than enough for three people.

Shaun, dressed mega coolly for a trip to the Odeon, in new blue jeans, a cream T-shirt and a brown suede jacket, reminds me of my end of the bedroom on an early autumn day, when the sun filters through the mesh curtains and sends mellow autumn hints and tints spiralling across the pale blue walls. A person's affinity to your bedroom, the most private and intimate part of your inner being, is quite a turn-on, you know. I *almost* fancy Shaun myself then, till I notice Arabella glowering in the dark, and I curb my embryonic desires and glue my eyes to the film.

There's something especially dreamy and poetic about Shaun this evening though, as if he's not quite sitting next to Arabella chomping noisily on her popcorn, but is off somewhere, penning a verse or painting a picture. Instead of being on a total lust drive, he's just simmering gently and doesn't make any attempt to inch his way up Arabella's thigh until at least three-quarters of the way through the film.

Disaster strikes as soon as we step out of the Odeon. Right in the middle of Clarendon Street, with no prior warning, Arabella finishes with Shaun.

"It's over, Shaun," she says.

"What have I done?" Shaun whimpers.

"Nothing. It's just over, that's all."

Now Arabella, for all her beauty and femininity, has never been known for her subtlety. "Over" means "Over" to her. No room for ifs or buts or whys or wherefores, or let's try again in a week. No room for any grey patches to creep in and blur her perfectly formed black-and-white picture of one boyfriend zooming out of her life, and a new one zooming in. But for Shaun, who has quite a few grey patches, which is why I think of an Impressionist painting whenever I look at him, "Over" doesn't mean what it does in the dictionary: at an end; finished. He keeps adding bits which don't bear any correlation to its meaning, like: "What, over until Monday, Arry?" or "Over? You don't mean it, Arry?" or "Over? For how long?". And without good reason too, because in my entire experience of living with Arabella, she has *never* finished with a boy and had him back. She has *always* moved straight on to the next one.

Shaun keeps watering down the meaning of "Over" till he's blue in the face. The more he waters it down, the more irritated Arabella gets. "OVER, OVER, OVER, Shaun. OVER means *OVER!*" she cries.

Poor boy, he's asking for it.

In astrology (which I'm interested in because it gives a slant on people's personalities which, if based on the exact time of their birth, is uncannily accurate) the elements of Fire and Water do not mix. They're a NO GO combination. I mean, in terms of sex, there's probably no better combination than Fire and Water (which is Aries, Leo and Sagittarius versus Pisces, Cancer and Scorpio) because water thrown on fire makes things very, very steamy indeed.

8

And judging from Arabella and Shaun behind the wheelie bins the other day, I can't argue with that. But personality-wise, don't even go there. Fire will burn delicate Water something rotten, and delicate Water will just put the dampers on all Fire's large, grandiose schemes. Arabella is Fire (Leo) and Shaun is Water (Pisces). Need I say more? Not really. But I'll just add that I am Virgo (Earth) because I was born after Arabella (and just after the cusp), which makes my ideal mate my opposite sign – Pisces.

When I look at Shaun next, he's trembling. It must be the shock of Arabella telling him it's over between them. It's then that Jung's anima pops up in him like a mermaid rising from the sea: tears well up in his eyes and plop onto the pavement. He tries to shield his eyes from us but it's obvious he's *very* upset. Arabella stalks off (probably cos she feels guilty), and even though I'm programmed to follow her, I can't just leave Shaun crying in the middle of the street with all the canoodling couples gawping at him; I must get him somewhere private. So, I grab his arm and usher him into the back of the Odeon foyer, where it's dark and there aren't so many people, and offer him the only bit of straggly loo roll I have. Fortunately, the film wasn't a weepy, so it's clean.

"Don't worry, Shaun," I say. "Arabella's always doing that to boys."

Something in what I say, or the way I say it, makes him sob good and proper then, right on my shoulder. I comfort him for a moment and then charge into the night after Arabella.

Chapter Two

It is May half-term: six weeks since Arabella split with Shaun, five-and-a-half since she took up with her new boyfriend, Alex. We're on holiday in Devon, basking on a sun-soaked beach. The sky is cloudless turquoise, the waves are swishing and swooshing hypnotically, the surf is crunching and crackling. Mum is lying beside me, reading *Woman and Home*. Bruno is next to her, snoring on a beach towel, his face pressed into the sand. Arabella is in the rock pools, searching for crabs.

I cannot settle to my book of Romantic Poetry, even though I've been looking forward to reading it for weeks. I cannot settle because there's something wrong with Arabella. I put out my twin feelers and pick up her pain. Then I rise from my towel and tiptoe across the sand to her. Tiptoeing is the only way to approach her, as charging up will make her back away like a defensive animal. I just hope she'll talk to me after nearly three days of being silent.

Now, I think I prefer bold, brazen Arabella to this shy, wimpy girl cowering over the rock pool like an all-too-familiar reflection of myself. She doesn't say a word, just crouches over the pool as though it's her only safe harbour. When a mother trails past with a toddler and a bucket, she folds her arms across her chest and shivers. What's so scary about a mother and a toddler crossing the sands, I wonder.

"Remember when we caught that enormous crab off Woolacombe beach, Arry, and you wanted to take it home in a bucket but changed your mind and let it go? That was a beautiful moment, watching it paddle away, wasn't it?"

She nods and scoops her hands through the water. In the end, I get sick of waiting for the miracle of her voice and wander back to my towel to read Wordsworth.

That evening the four of us huddle round the fire in our holiday cottage (the evenings are still cold, despite it being May) and munch cheese on toast. At eleven p.m. the latch of my bedroom door lifts, and I see Arabella standing barefoot in the doorway, her white nightie billowing around her. She crosses the room and climbs into bed with me. Her feet are frozen blocks of ice, which accidentally on purpose nudge my ankles; her whole body is stiff with fear. I stretch out my hand and she grips it hard.

Just *what* is making her so peculiar? I don't say a word. The best psychology with someone terrified is not to say a word: just give them encouraging, non-verbal prompts. I squeeze her arm. BINGO, she speaks!

"I think I might have done something terrible, Sadie. I think I have but I'm not sure."

I think murder, arson, rape, bullying, incest, theft, and all the terrible things a human being can get up to.

"What?" I say.

"Something happened."

"What?"

"Oh, God," she groans from under the duvet. "Can't you guess? You're my twin. You're *supposed* to know everything about me!"

I do guess then, but only because she sits bolt upright, puts on the bedside lamp and gives me one of her totally transparent looks. Her face is bright red from too little sun cream, her eyes blood red from too much crying.

"I think I'm pregnant!"

"Nonsense," I say, because for all that fondling with Shaun behind telegraph poles, this is a preposterous idea.

"I haven't had my period. I must be!"

But it's girls like me who get themselves pregnant: girls too green and innocent to know how far you can go with a boy before it becomes dangerous. Not girls like Arabella. She's all bodily knowledge and sophistication. Besides, she has just spent the best part of a month studying the ins and outs of the human reproductive system and is going to become a doctor.

She sobs hysterically and clutches me. Then she does her compromise bit, which I *hate*, and makes me swear on our Golden Retriever's life not to say anything to Mum or Bruno, or any person in the human race for that matter. Either I care far too much about Sammy or Arabella's hold on me is lessening, but I just can't swear on his life. So, I just swear not to say a word, after which she pleads for my advice.

"What on earth did you get up to with Shaun?" I ask.

"Things," she says, "and with Alex, not Shaun. Early on."

"What kind of *things*?"

"*Things!*" she repeats, jabbing me in the calf with her toenail.

I can't advise her. It's the one occasion I'm lost for ideas, other than the obvious one of tell Mum and get a pregnancy test. I keep my promise and don't breathe a word, but by the following Monday Arabella's period still hasn't come, and Mum and Bruno know everything. Instantly, without even digesting the possibility of a new addition to our family, Mum marches Arabella first to the chemist for a pregnancy test and then to the GP for a check-up, and Bruno just goes ballistic, hurling empty Tupperware containers around, kicking Sammy's food bowl to pieces, slamming doors and stomping around upstairs till he nearly comes through the ceiling, and demanding over and over to know the name of the boy involved. Anyone would think he was Arabella's dad!

That's the day I decide Bruno is creepily protective of Arabella. I mean, if it were the other way round and *I* thought *I* was pregnant, no way would he be in such a state.

Arabella is sick with relief. Her test is negative, and she isn't pregnant but anaemic. I let her share my bed for the next two nights, just until she feels secure again, and Mum puts her on a course of iron tablets and lectures her on what *not* to do with boys.

***

Bruno has left! He and Mum had a flaming row, re the pregnancy scare, and he has sped off into the night in his camper van. So now we're a happy, contented family again: Mum, me, Arabella and Sammy. For the first time in two years I can relax, chill and nestle up to the bosom of my family, gently rocked in the hammock of their love.

The phantom pregnancy has turned out to be a blessing in disguise: Mum is calm and the knot in her stomach has unravelled, and Arabella has turned boy-shy and become incredibly nice with it, which means I no longer have to tag along with her and her useless boyfriends, and she waits on me, hand and foot. The new routine is that we have supper early (usually made by Arabella) and snuggle up to Mum while we watch our favourite TV programmes, and then we do our homework. Bath time is different too. Instead of listening to Radio One, Arabella recites Latin names of muscles *endlessly*: rectus abdominis, erector spinae, latissimus dorsi, teres major, teres minor, gluteus minimus, gluteus maximus… When I use the bath after her, I find these strange muscular shapes traced on the steamy tiles. She's hell-bent on becoming a doctor and says Dr Roberts has completely inspired her.

BOMBSHELL NUMBER THREE (following on from **BOMBSHELL NUMBER ONE** – Arabella jilting Shaun – and **BOMBSHELL NUMBER TWO** – the phantom pregnancy): SHAUN HAS ASKED ME OUT… and… I'VE ACCEPTED!

I'm all in a jitter because I didn't see it coming, not in a hundred years! I thought he only had eyes for Arabella. But no, it seems he has turned those dewy green orbs on me for a change. I haven't a clue what to wear. Arabella has offered me her entire wardrobe, but I've rejected the lot, bar one slinky top, which I may or may not wear.

For the bottom half, I'm going into Guildford *alone* and choosing something *without* her help. I'm so excited and proud of myself. Even if I come away with the worst bottom half in the world, it'll still be *my* choice, and that's what counts. And if Shaun's as nice as he's cracked up to be, he'll like me whatever I put on.

Still, I can't help wondering WHY ME? Was it because I was kind to him in the Odeon that time? I hope not, cos you can't build a love affair on kindness alone.

Then it occurs to me why Shaun has asked me out. It's called the law of dominance and submission and dictates that when someone or something moves out of the foreground of a situation, whoever or whatever is in the background comes to the foreground. Natural law determines this. Ten weeks ago, Arabella was very much in the foreground, and I was very much in the background where Shaun was concerned. But since finishing with Shaun and becoming obsessed first with Alex and then with becoming a doctor, Arabella has receded into the background, and I've come forward.

The tables have turned. Our roles have reversed. Boys (and one in particular) have started to notice ME! And this is how it all got going. I am coming along the pavement from St Helen's, which is my school, and Shaun is coming in the opposite direction from St Christopher's, which is his. At first, I don't see him because I am busy controlling the chocolate cake I've just made in Food Technology.

Shaun doesn't see me either, and we smack straight into each other. The cake goes flying, Shaun leaps into the air and catches it, and our eyes meet. Without lenses, Shaun's eyes are the most perfect spangle of orange, green and aquamarine. Briefly, I feel like I'm swimming in the Great Barrier Reef.

The shock of colliding with Shaun is almost as great as the tizzy he puts me in when I look into his eyes. But Shaun being Shaun, he just laughs quietly, cracks a joke and asks me if any bones are broken. I stutter and splutter and eventually find I am able to formulate a reasonably coherent answer, which communicates I am unharmed and have made a stupendous chocolate cake, which I am taking home to share with my family.

Perhaps I should invite him back to the house to share a slice with us, I think.

BUT NO.

HOME = ARABELLA = SHAUN + ARABELLA = DANGER.
Instantly, I eradicate the thought.

"How's Arabella?" he asks.

"Fine. *Very* happy to be single," I say, deliberately laying it on thick. "She's engrossed in the endocrine system. She wants to be a doctor, you know. Any message you'd like me to give her?"

"No," Shaun replies, his face crumpling with disappointment.

There is a long, tense silence, which I calculate will only end when Shaun is distracted by something on the street. I'm right. A black poodle, minus a lead and a mistress, trots towards us, and Shaun steps aside to let it pass. See, he's even polite to dogs!

"Fancy coming to the park tonight, Sadie? I'm bored at home," he suddenly says.

Deliberately, I don't say "yes" or "no". In this way I get to be a bit of a mystery woman, and Shaun gets to fancy me a little bit more. That's according to law number two – the law of openness and secrecy – which dictates that if a girl spills out everything about herself ("Yes, Shaun, I *am* desperate to go to the park with you. Yes, I *am* desperate for a snog. Yes, I *am* desperate for you to put your hand up my skirt and finger my thigh and other bits, like you did with Arabella. Yes, Shaun, I *am* DESPERATE!"), the boy is bound to run a mile and never come back. Playing it cool, hedging, umming and ahhing (but not *so* much he loses interest) and emitting an irresistible air of insouciance, are bound to have the desired effect and, in my case, make Shaun forget all about Arabella and drag me to the park, there and then, for an instant snog, chocolate cake and all.

I gulp, trying to manufacture this mysterious air of insouciance, but a huge red lump, the size of a ginormous gobstopper, sticks out of my throat – a tell-tale sign, if ever there was one, not of insouciance but of downright *terror*!

"I'll meet you at the end of the road at four forty-five, then," Shaun says.

I charge home, the cake slipping and sliding everywhere, lay the table, slice up three pieces of cake, scoff my piece, wash my hands, wash my plate, clean my teeth, change my clothes, write a note, check my phone and charge out again.

Shaun is late.

Alarm bells clang in my head. Then he appears around the corner, in exactly the same clothes, smiling. He is tall and lean and an exceptionally fast walker. I have to jog to keep up with him. By the time we get to the park entrance, he's practically lapped me.

All the time we are in the park, I am praying Shaun will take me to the arboretum, where, in the current month of June, birds sing, sap oozes, small animals procreate, blossoms burst forth and willows and birches cascade, lattice-like, over human heads, like a marriage bower. *The arboretum is the most romantic place on earth.* But he doesn't and instead chooses a seat in full public view, near the children's swings, where there's a load of dog mess. He buys me an ice cream, which I can hardly stomach after all the chocolate cake and a fresh bout of indigestion and the smell of dog poo wafting my way. Still, I try to make out I'm enjoying it.

Arabella's psychic presence in the park is awesome. As I lick my Mr Whippy, I feel her plonk herself right between us. I try to wriggle nearer to Shaun and forget she's there, but she uses her magic power to push me back to my original spot, i.e. sixty inches from him. That's the terrible thing about twins: the one twin can be with the other twin even when she's not welcome. They can make their spirit felt to each other at the most inappropriate times, and Arabella, being especially clever and more than a bit jealous of my friendship with Shaun (even though she doesn't want him herself), is ace at this.

At ten past six, Shaun wants to go. I throw the remains of my Mr Whippy into the bin and walk (or rather, run) alongside him. *Our first date has been a total disaster, and my world is falling apart.* We've hardly talked at all, which is taking the mystery thing *way too far*, and there hasn't even been a warm-up to a snog. I don't think Shaun will ask me out again.

BOMBSHELL NUMBER FOUR – HE DOES! THE FOLLOWING THURSDAY!

***

At birth, Arabella was given a four-syllable name – Ar-a-bell-a – and I was given a two-syllable name – Sad-ie. Sometimes, on a bad day, I am just one-syllable – Sad. And that's what I am today, on Saturday, midway through June: sad because Arabella is reclaiming her power. Sick to death of examining diagrams of the male body, she wants to get back to exploring it for real. In other words, she's not boy-shy any more, and that's bad news for me.

On the other hand, I'm not in Arabella's shadow so much any more and have a real boyfriend of my own (even if he *is* her cast-off). And I'm easily Arabella's equal in surface area, if nothing else, so why should I vanish just because she expands? Restlessly, I circle my end of the bedroom three times in succession, as an ancient tribal affirmation of my progressive power. Halfway through my third perambulation, I see Shaun sauntering up our garden path. Totally agitated, I nearly embark on a fourth perambulation, but no, that would be bad luck. Three is lucky: Father, Son and Holy Spirit. I *must* stick to three.

The bell rings and Arabella goes to the front door. I expect some kind of mass explosion as she opens it because this is the first time they have faced each other since she gave him the push. Any second now, Shaun could be scampering back down our garden path with his nose severely out of joint. I open the bedroom door a crack (don't know *why* I'm being so cautious – I *am* his girlfriend, after all) and creep downstairs.

Arabella has let Shaun in, and they are sitting opposite each other in our sun-filled conservatory. Shaun looks white with nerves, and from his light blue shirt and aromatic aftershave (neither of which he had on for *our* date), I guess has made a special effort to look and smell good. Arabella just looks Goddess. Sickening, isn't it, that she can look *this* good when she has been skipping meals and shut up for days in an airless room, regurgitating page after page of dry biological facts? I mean, she *should* have small, shrunken eyes, and a nasty, creased brow from too much academic stress, and skin that is drawn and blotchy and pimply. Any normal person would. But Arabella's beauty seems to thrive on hardship. She looks *exquisite*!

"Shaun just popped round to say Hi," she says, giving me a smile so obviously insincere I wonder why I don't just leave there and then. "Make us a cuppa, Sad," she adds.

How dare she call me Sad in front of Shaun!

"No!" I exclaim.

She shrugs, tosses her damp, tousled hair and shoots Shaun and me a glance which says: "well, I can hardly make one myself and leave you alone together, can I?"

I smile to myself, not openly, but right in the pit of my stomach, where no-one can see it. But then Arabella does something unbelievable, which I haven't planned for, and it sends me reeling. She unlocks her legs, gets up, strolls over to Shaun and implants a large, sloppy kiss on his cheek. I'm flabbergasted! So is Shaun for a second, before his face breaks into a grin of shameful delight. Then, gloating with triumph, she wafts from the conservatory, leaving me on my own with him.

Water builds and throbs behind my eyes; I daren't look at Shaun or it will burst out like a perforated dam. I make a show of scratching my right temple, thereby fringing my eyes from him, and turn my gaze in the direction of our back garden, pretending I have an informed knowledge and appreciation of early summer flowers and shrubs. My eyes wash over the grass, alighting by accident on the old, lichen-covered garden chair my dad used to sit on. It's the final straw. I rush out of the conservatory, into the garden and collapse in a soggy mass behind the compost heap.

Chapter Three

It's sleeting outside in hard diagonal stripes across the horizon, making me think more of winter than of summer. If Shaun wants me, sleet or no sleet, he'll be underneath the lamp post on Walker Street, because that's where we've arranged to meet for our second date.

I can't decide whether to go to meet Shaun, and my whole body pulsates with indecision. After what happened in the conservatory the other day, chances are he won't even be there. But if I don't go, I'll never know. So, I act positively, striding purposefully in the direction of Walker Street and, through the lashing sleet, spot Shaun, bedraggled and shivering beneath the lamp post.

We dive into the nearest café and order a large plate of chips. Shaun is ravenously hungry, evident in the way he stuffs several chips into his mouth all at once. Then he gives me a funny look across the table: a strange, inscrutable look I haven't seen before and can't work out. I smile sweetly at him, in the hope that this will bring some clarity to his expression.

"We might as well go back to my place to practise," he says.

I gulp, seize one more chip and stuff it into my mouth, avoiding all eye contact with him for fear of having too much of a good thing and drowning in his ocean's depths. The way he says, "my place", you'd think he was twenty-one, not sixteen! There is something tantalisingly adult about his voice, and the way he thrusts his hands into his pockets and leans back in his seat, waiting for me to respond.

"I don't have my violin," I say.

"No prob. You can use Grandpa's. It's a Strad, you know."

"OK," I murmur, and off we go.

Shaun's house, on the northern edge of town, is all polished wooden floors and low-hanging crystal chandeliers and large, round oak tables with dimly lit lamps, illuminating sprays of freshly cut flowers, and William Morris embossed tiles surrounding dark, sunken Victorian fireplaces. I gasp as I step into the hall, the library, the sitting room. A lady in a cream silk dress drifts past us on the stairs – a ghost maybe, but more likely with her long ebony hair and pale green eyes, Shaun's mum.

"We're going to practise in the attic," Shaun says.

"OK, darling," the lady murmurs, sliding away.

The attic is hot and creaky, low-ceilinged and dusty, and Shaun can only just stand up in it. He says, though, that it's the only place to make music without disturbing the whole house. He hands me a bulging violin case, with the initials JW woven along the side. Looking at it, I feel like a criminal about to ransack someone's house – guilty but voracious for the goods inside. I unzip the case and pull out the violin, while Shaun watches me intently. This is surely heaven: a Stradivarius between my hands, Shaun's eyes all over me. I pluck a string and pull the bow from the case, then ease the instrument under my chin, stroking it into expression.

"Let's go for it!" Shaun cries, blasting on his sax and nearly deafening me.

My violin whines and hums pathetically beneath the blast of his sax, but then I get into my stride, streaking string on string more and more confidently, cutting and streaking and weaving between the deep rumble of Shaun's notes, like lightning through a thunder-torn sky.

"That was brill!" Shaun says when we finish.

So brill, I don't want to spoil it by doing something stupid. Ever so carefully, I lay down the Stradivarius on top of the case and, with my best air of insouciance, wander over to the attic window, where clusters of cobwebs and dead wasps cling to the glass and the light struggles to penetrate, and just stand there, with my back to Shaun, straining to see out. The plan is Shaun will sidle over, slide his arms around my waist, spin me round and kiss me.

Only, this doesn't happen, and the more I strain to see the Surrey countryside through the murky panes, the more I just see my own face reflected in the glass, and the more I try *not* to see my face, the more I *do* see it, the way suddenly you can't see the telly programme you're watching for the huge cactus stuck on top of the telly. I'm not a pretty sight after all the rain and the fusty, musty heat of the attic. Instead of forming soft, romantic curls around my face, my hair is frizzing like an overused Brillo pad, and my cheeks are all puffy. I can see hints of Arabella in my reflection – the outline of her chin, the smooth, broad sweep of her forehead – but they are only hints that tease and goad me with the notion of unrealised beauty, of perfection never reached. Anger and resentment fill my heart. I try to banish Arabella from my head, but she lodges herself there, and the next thing I know Shaun is right beside me, staring at my reflection too.

"You're nothing like Arabella, are you?" he says dreamily, as if he's lost in wonder at the vast difference between us. "I mean, for twins, you're *very different*."

"So people say," I reply, trying not to sound miffed.

"I mean, if Arry were here now" (and he lets out this weird giggle), "we wouldn't be making music and we wouldn't just be standing here… we'd be… well, you know…"

He stops giggling when he sees the hurt on my face. Yes, I know: they'd be all over each other, going at it like a couple of hares on a fresh March morning.

"You miss her, don't you? You wish Arabella were here with you and not me."

I don't really mean to say this – it just comes out – and it knocks Shaun for six. He jerks back and rubs his forehead fiercely, as if he's really suffering.

"No, you don't understand, Sadie! I don't mean I prefer Arry to you, or that I want her to be here. I just mean as twins you're very different, when twins are usually alike."

It's a tactful answer and, if I don't read *too* much into it, kind of makes sense. I cool it and smile softly to show Shaun I forgive him and am prepared to let the subject of Arabella drop. Only, he won't let me. He's pacing the attic floor, wild with excitement. His face has changed from that of a normal, good looking sixteen-year-old guy to one high on drugs!

"You're *totally* different! You hang back while Arry dives in. You want to talk while she wants to grope. It's nice. It feels like you want to get to know me a bit. It feels like you're not just after one thing."

Only then do I summon the courage to turn away from my own reflection and look directly at Shaun, and *boy* is it a big moment! Shaun is gazing at me ocean, stars, sun and moon. Right now, there isn't a planet in the solar system that his eyes don't mirror. He has just paid me the biggest compliment a boy can pay a girl – bigger than you've got a sexy smile or incredible tits, because in admitting that he likes me *as I am*, he has glimpsed my essence. He has seen beyond my Brillo pad hair to my *soul*.

"Talk to me, Sadie," he says very, very softly.

But what can I say in such a world-stopping moment? I stare at him dumbly, wishing I could find the words.

Then, as Shaun raises his hand to wipe the dust from the windowpane and flick away the dead wasps, our little fingers brush in a moment of pure magic. My own reflection vanishes, and Surrey bursts into view.

***

After my magical experience with Shaun up in his attic, I've decided that my life is to be a journey towards wholeness. By this, I mean I will aim to be less like the supermodel in the skin ad and more like my true self. I will develop my own identity and do my own thing. In fact, I've already started. So much has changed in the space of a few months: I no longer trail behind Arabella and her boyfriends; I wear my own clothes, not hers; I have my own boyfriend, and I have just moved into my own bedroom. I am emerging into the woman I want to be.

Every now and again though, I find myself slipping back to the girl I used to be and, once I've slipped, it takes a hell of a lot of scrabbling about in the mud to get myself out again, and I end up wondering if this independence thing is a bit of a fantasy and I should just settle for being sad old Sad, the left arm of Arabella's right.

One Saturday in early July, I get home after a blissful afternoon with Shaun. The sun has shone all day. We've paddled in the river and sunbathed in a cornfield, and at five p.m. we wave goodbye to each other. Sammy greets me at the front door, his golden mane rippling in the summer breeze, his mood of majestic imperturbability blending perfectly with my own mood. I run my hands through his coat, go into the kitchen, pour two glasses of freshly squeezed orange juice, one for Mum, one for me, and take them out to sip under the shade of the willow tree.

Mum approves massively of me going out with Shaun. She says when Shaun and Arabella were an item, it wasn't Shaun but Arabella who was the worry, and she trusts I won't give her the same number of sleepless nights. I don't like to disappoint her by saying I've recently had a finger-brushing moment of pure magic with Shaun up in his attic, and from little things big things come. So, I just nod in agreement, stretch back in my deck chair, sip my orange juice and generally drink in the peace and tranquillity of the afternoon; for a full five minutes, until an unfamiliar sound pierces the air, and it's not Mrs Hodges caterwauling over the garden fence or Sammy seeing off a cat, but the high-pitched squeak of Arabella's new trainers making contact with the grass.

She appears beside us under the willow tree and plonks herself at my feet. She's hardly in the kind of mood that befits a glorious summer's day. For one thing, she's scowling hideously; for another, she has gone into monosyllabic mode where you can hardly drag a thing out of her, though Mum tries her best.

"Had a good afternoon, Arry?"

"Ish," Arabella mutters.

"Been to town?"

"Yep."

"Buy anything?"

"Nope."

"See anyone?"

"Nope."

"Have any plans for tonight?"

"Nope."

"Like anything in particular for supper?"

"Whatever."

And that's the sum of their conversation: twenty-three words from Mum, five-and-a-half from Arry. I try to ease things along by cracking the odd joke, but it's too hot and too much like hard work, and anyway, Mum's patience is wearing thin. She knows Arabella has taken up with Alex again; she knows how she feels about that – *seriously unimpressed* – and she knows, without proof, she can't do a thing about it.

"Teenagers!" she exclaims and stalks off to cook supper.

Arabella stares mysteriously at the horizon. When she wants, she can be as remote as Ben Nevis on a foggy day. But just as you imagine she cannot be scaled and will never be reached, the fog around her clears and she shrinks to the size of a hillock, then to a grassy incline and suddenly she's back in our garden, a neat little molehill, right there in your face. I try to get up, but she wedges me to the chair with the rod of her spine. She's only slight, but the muscles of her back grip me like an octopus's arms.

"Don't go, Sadie. I need to ask you something."

I sink back in the canvas, prepared at least to hear her out. She twists her neck to look round at me, wraps her slender arms around my legs and wheedles in her most wheedling voice ever:

"Do me a favour and come out with Alex and me tomorrow. Just this once… *please*."

Her appeal is weak and pathetic, like the cry of a baby gull pushed from its nest. Confusion and indecision rage within me. I've arranged to see Shaun tomorrow. The weather promises to be fine and we're going upstream to spot otters. Arabella is asking me to sacrifice the thing I want to do *most*.

"*Please… Sadie…*" she wheedles.

Then her whole body goes limp, and she collapses against me, and for one senseless moment I imagine her to be dead. Shaun, otters, boat trips, sun-dappled trees and rivers all dwindle into insignificance in the face of life without Arabella.

"OK, OK," I say, desperately. "But once and once *only*!"

"You're a star, Sadie. A total star!"

And, quite miraculously, she comes back to life.

What all this means, of course, is that Arabella is pushing me deeper and deeper into the mud, and I'm letting her push me there. *Her* artful manipulation and *my* overactive imagination are lethal, otherwise I'd never have supposed her dead at my feet, never have given in to her request and never be in this mess now. Worst of all, even though I can see exactly what she's playing at, I still let her do it.

Chapter Four

I phone Shaun to cancel the otter trip. He's laid-back about it and doesn't ask a single question, which makes me a bit uneasy. I mean, shouldn't he be really jealous and demand to know where I'm going, with whom and why? Then I lie to Mum by saying Arry and I will be spending the whole of Sunday in Guildford shopping centre, which makes me hate Arabella and hate myself.

That night I have a mini, borderline major, crisis about Shaun. We've been together for a while now and still haven't snogged, whereas Arabella and Shaun snogged on day one of going out and rapidly moved on to other things. OK, so my relationship with Shaun is extra tender, extra sweet and slow-maturing, like sun-ripened grain, and he wants to get to know me a bit. But if we go much slower, we'll be dead! Most days we just listen to jazz albums and stare dreamily into each other's eyes. There hasn't been a single episode of finger-creeping in the direction of my skirt, let alone under it and up it!

What can I do? I feel so powerless. Can't he tell I'm nuts about him? I don't wear that scratchy push-up bra or plaster my lips in that vanilla gunk for nothing, you know, Shaun. I'm a skin-sensitive, semi-diabetic for God's sake! But all I get is: "Hi, Sadie. You look nice. Fancy a cuppa?" Never: "You look dead sexy, Sadie. Up to my room NOW!" Perhaps the plain truth is that Shaun doesn't fancy me. But why ask me out in the first place then, and why look into my eyes as though I had eyes to die for?

By the time I've finished agonising about Shaun, I'm a bath of perspiration and have to search for a clean T-shirt and shorts in the laundry cupboard. I rifle through layers and layers of Arabella's thongs before getting to my shorts. I close the cupboard door and pad back across the landing, automatically pausing outside Arabella's door. Half of me wants to pour out my heart about Shaun (Arabella *is* my twin after all, and I should be able to tell her *anything*), and the other half wants to hide away, hoping for a miracle.

Once, I watched a movie called *Demonic Nights*. It made my blood run cold. I sent an email of complaint to the film regulators, saying it should be an eighteen, not a twelve. I forgot about it then, until riding around in Alex's black Escort on Sunday afternoon it suddenly dawns on me that Alex is the exact replica of Count Weimar, who experiments on young girls in his black-tiled laboratory and then dumps them in the local lake: the same thin, mean lips; the same dark, menacing eyes that *only* look at you sideways; the same pointed fingernails, encrusted with dirt and specks of blood. I need to find out where Alex is taking us – FAST.

"It's a surprise," he grunts.

We drive for miles, during which time Arabella falls into a deep sleep (I'm terrified she's been drugged), and I'm left with Alex hurtling along at breakneck speed, mumbling Eminem lyrics under his breath. It's a nightmarish fifteen minutes of careering down spooky country lanes too narrow and overgrown to take a car, at the end of which a low-roofed derelict cottage, with upper and lower windows smashed in and a vandalised name board turned upside down, awaits our entrance.

Crashing up to its walls, Alex turns off the engine and just stares at the cottage, transfixed, before flicking the keys from the ignition, climbing out of the car and striding around the side of the building anticlockwise. Seconds later, he's back, looking weirdly pleased with himself, and jangles the keys at Arry to wake up.

I have to prod Arabella in the ribs to get her to stir. She rubs her eyes, makes little ooh aah sounds at the cottage and smiles goofily at Alex, like he's just delivered her a dream home straight off the top of a biscuit tin. That's when I seriously question if this is my twin of former days, who recited Latin names in the bath and aspired to be a doctor. *That* twin had a brain.

While Alex is fumbling with the door lock, I try to persuade Arry not to go into the cottage.

"This place is seriously weird, Arry. I don't think we should go in. I think we should make a run for it."

She looks at me as if I've just won the jackpot and turned the lot down.

"What do you think I am, crazy or something?"

"No, but I don't like the look of this place, and I don't trust Alex, either."

"Suit yourself, Sadie. *I'm* going in!"

Reluctantly, I follow her into the cottage. There are no dismembered bodies under the stairs, or books on mass murderers, or anything obviously evil about the place. Actually, things seem pretty normal. By which I mean a few Stephen King novels litter the bookshelves, and a Francis Bacon print hangs skew-whiff over the fireplace, like you might find in any house. In fact, the weirdest thing about the cottage is its bareness: no carpet on the floor; no signs of present or recent habitation; no homely touches, like a bundle of knitting or a pair of slippers pushed under a chair.

The sofas are bright orange and full of holes, with bits of sponge sticking out of them, most probably eaten by moths or rats, and there's a book on rat keeping propped up against the fireplace. And that's about as weird as it gets. Still, I'm praying Alex won't give us a guided tour. There's something creepy about the atmosphere here and this feeling gets stronger the closer I go to the staircase.

I needn't worry cos Alex is in no mood to play estate agents. He's in no mood for me, either. He's here for one reason only – to get Arry up to that bedroom – and from the lustful glint in his eye, *no-one* and *nothing* is going to stop him.

"Faz? Where the hell are you? Faz?"

Alex's voice resounds around the cottage, fading to a spooky reverberation.

28

"*Faz... Faz...*"

Judging by all the holes around the place, I guess Faz must be a long, furry creature, which any second will come scuttling from its hideaway and up my legs. I'm wrong, because on the fifth boom of "Faz?", a teenage boy, whom I'd swear is Alex's twin brother (were it not for the fact that Alex doesn't have one), pokes his long, indented face through the bannisters, making me jump out of my skin.

"Thought I wasn't around, did you?"

"I *was* wondering," Alex drawls morosely. "This is Arry and her sister, Sad."

"*Sadie!*" I screech.

The boy gives me a pitiful glance, before slinking up to me and inspecting my face closely.

"Nice eyes, all right face. Pity we can't do a swap, though."

Smiling freakishly, Faz exposes a higgledy-piggledy set of yellow teeth, between which bits of his dinner have got stuck. He smells strange, of putty or something, like he could have been doing some DIY in the bathroom before we arrived, and the smell makes me lurch sideways.

"Get us a drink then, mate," Alex drones. "Let's get the party going."

Flicking up a loose floorboard with his foot, Faz scoops four cans of lager from a hole in the floor and passes one to Alex, one to Arabella and one to me. I give mine straight back to him.

"Arabella and I don't drink alcohol. We're underage," I say.

I try to get Arabella to back me up, but she's as red as a raspberry, has her eyes fixed on the hole in the floor and won't look at me. I wonder why!

"Fair enough," Alex snaps and he snatches the can off Arabella, yanks off the aluminium ring and pushes it back into her hand, the lager slopping everywhere. It's Alex's way of trying to be macho and prove he's top dog in his cottage. Then, acting like I don't even exist, he grabs Arabella's hand and tugs her towards the spiral staircase, and I watch her spiral round and round the stairs, like a floppy rag doll, till all I can see are her thin little heels sticking through the gap in the top stair and being dragged away.

I reckon if I stay calm, I've a seven in ten chance of getting out of here alive (and getting help), but if I panic, I've zero chance of anything.

Faz is on the sofa now, wedged between all the spongy bits, plucking bits of foam from the cushions and leering at me from under lashes as thick and black as tarantula legs. Suddenly, he starts patting this wodge of cushion, like he wants me to cosy up beside him. *No way am I doing that!*

When I don't, he leaps off the foam towards me. I'm terrified he's going to pin me to the floor and start doing loads of disgusting things, but he flies straight past me, mumbling stuff about bladders and pees and bladders the size of peas and vanishes into a back room. I hear a sharp, shooting sound, like a jet from a water pistol being aimed at a wall and *that*'s when I make a run for it – out through the bashed-in front door, around the side of Alex's black Escort and straight down the dirt track, running like I've *never, ever* run in my life, till I hit the road.

All the time I'm running, I'm expecting Faz's claw-like hand to grip me round the neck and drag me back to the cottage, just like the hand of Count Weimar's assistant in *Demonic Nights*. But there's no hand, no Faz, nothing for miles: just a long, empty track, fading away behind me. Twenty-five minutes later I'm at the main road and nearly dead with exhaustion. I can't believe I'm out of there. I can't believe I've escaped. I can't believe I've left Arabella in the grip of a monster!

***

"Where's Arry?" is the first thing Mum asks.

"With Zoe in ZARA," I mumble, turning my face from her in shame.

30

I must be crazy! Why don't I just tell Mum the truth? Arabella could be dead by now, or pregnant with one of Count Weimar's babies, and then I'd have some explaining to do. I lock myself in the bathroom, climb onto the bath and scour the street for Alex's black Escort. If she's not back within the hour, I'll tell Mum *everything* and we'll go get her.

But she is – within half an hour, actually – and looking so fit and healthy and pleased with herself, my relief comes out in a spurt of rage.

"What the hell were you doing dragging me into the woods with your weirdo boyfriend and his git of a mate? Anything could have happened!"

"I didn't know Faz was going to be there," she snorts. "Alex said he'd invited some friends. I thought it would do you good, instead of being lonely with lonesome Shaun all the time. You're too sheltered, Sadie. You need to get out, LIVE, see the REAL world, instead of huddling up to Mum and Shaun all the time. I mean, has Shaun actually snogged you yet? He's a fast worker, you know, but it's like he's found slow motion with you. Maybe he doesn't fancy you after all."

I slap her then, sharply across the top of her head. Well, clip is probably a better word because it doesn't come out as a full-blown slap. I know violence is a terrible thing and I shouldn't have done it, but *she* drove me to it. Then I pick up the pink hand towel that has slipped off the bath, put it back in place and march out, leaving Arabella snivelling over the wash basin.

We don't speak for two days. The atmosphere in the house is gruesome; far from cutting it with a knife, you could hack it with an axe. Mum keeps demanding an explanation from us both, which neither of us wants to give, which only makes her demand even more. In the end, I present Mum with fragments of the truth, like: "after the shops we went round to a friend's place and there were some people there I didn't like, so I left and Arry stayed on." I don't add that we were in this spooky cottage with weird Alex and even weirder Faz because that would really freak Mum out.

At the end of day two, a text comes through to my bedroom.

Sorry, Sadie... so so sorry... I'm out here if you want to make up. Arry xx

And there she is, hovering outside my bedroom like an angel of light, emitting rays of love so pure and innocent they instantly melt all the guilt, pain, anger and resentment in my heart. Before I know it, we're hugging and making up, and she's telling me stuff she's *never, ever* told me before.

"I love him, Sadie. That's why I can't tell Mum – cos she'll stop me seeing him. He says when I'm eighteen, he wants us to get engaged."

Stunned silence from me.

"No, I mean it. I *love* Alex and he *loves* me. Just think, one day he'll be your brother-in-law."

But I don't want to think about it. Love... Alex... engagement... brother-in-law... when she's eighteen... It's my worst nightmare!

"Well, aren't you pleased?" Arabella whimpers.

"Sure," I say, disentangling myself from her hug and trying my best to look happy. "Sure, I'm pleased."

What else can I say? Go along with what Arry wants and there's a tiny chance one day she'll come to her senses and dump Alex. But go *against* what she wants and I'm doomed to a lifetime of Count Weimar's blood-curdling ways.

Alone, on my dad's lichen-covered garden seat late at night, I try to fathom the unfathomable: Arabella's love for Alex. Just *what* does she see in him? Just *what* does she fancy? Shaun's a billion times nicer, kinder, more intelligent *and* good looking, but the word love never crossed her lips with him, nor with any of the boys who came before him. The more I try to solve this mystery, the more mystified I am, till all I can conclude is that Arabella is in the grip of a dark, menacing force called Alex, the way Tess of the d'Urbervilles was in the grip of a dark, menacing force called Alec in Thomas Hardy's novel.

Each time I think of Arabella being led up that spiral staircase by Alex, I think of Tess being led into the woods by Alec. It's getting dark, the fog is swirling, the way ahead is murky and uncertain, but Alec knows what he wants and he's out to get it. He leads Tess into the undergrowth, like a lamb to the slaughter. When Tess comes out, her life has changed forever. It takes a whole novel for Alec's power to be broken, and this only happens when Tess kills him. Tess says she was "dazed" by Alec, and that's what Arabella is by Alex – dazed – so much she can't see what he's *really* like or what he's *doing* to her.

Chapter Five

It's the first day of the summer holidays and Mum is in a state of trepidation. Not surprisingly, as last year's holiday was a fiasco, and she keeps having flashbacks. It was supposed to be a dream holiday: two weeks of sizzling sun on the Costa Brava. But from the moment we got on the plane, to the moment we got off, things went wrong. I'll spare you the details, but, in short: a man spilt coffee over Bruno, and Bruno blew up. Arabella was air sick, but there were no bags to hand, and her sick went all over the seats, and we were squashed together in a minuscule apartment, next to a building site, with a trickle for a shower and a toilet no better than a hole in the ground.

Later, Mum told me all she wanted to do on that holiday was hide behind a Spanish rock. After all, it *was* the holiday Bruno wouldn't stop gibing her about her cellulite and refused to take his eyes off all the topless women on the beach. I'm glad Mum saw sense and booted him out. The trouble is, now that Bruno's gone and the house is as quiet as death during the day, she kids herself she wants him back. I say it's all in the mind – she doesn't like being lonely and Bruno filled the void, so she *thinks* she wants *him* back. I hope I'm right, because if it is Bruno she wants and not just a void-filler, it will be tough having him living here again.

So, on Mum's say-so, the first week of this summer holiday is to be constructive. Lolling around in the sun is out. I can't say I'm bothered. I'd much rather be *doing* something, but Arabella won't be able to stand it. In July and August, her entire raison d'être is to turn the colour of a date, and a shiny date at that, so Alex can lick and nibble her to his heart's content. She can't stand constructive or cultural, and Mum has just announced we're doing both – we're off to the National Gallery in London to see a Post-Impressionist exhibition.

"Urgh," Arabella groans, pretending to sick up her buttered croissant. "Sounds like a fun day out!"

Then, quite blatantly, she changes her tune.

"I mean, I'm sure the paintings are really interesting, but I was hoping to stay local to choose a pattern for my new skirt. Why don't you and Sadie go, Mum, and I'll stop here and make us a delicious pasta for supper?"

I know exactly what she's angling for and it's nothing to do with patterns or pasta. She wants the house to herself, so she and Alex can sprawl around like love sickies on Mum's new silk throw. The idea irritates the hell out of me.

"You can get a pattern any time," I say. "Mum has arranged this trip and you're coming. Anyway, I want supper in London."

Arabella shrugs, I beam encouragingly at Mum, and Mum's mind is made up.

"The train leaves in half an hour. Clean your teeth and jump in the car, girls."

If only it were that simple. Ten minutes before the train is due to pull out, Arabella is still applying her mascara, and no amount of yelling or coaxing from Mum and me can persuade her to bring her cosmetic bag with her, which means we make a mad dash to the station and Mum breaks the speed limit and nearly mows down a black cat. Not the luckiest start!

Fortunately, the train soothes our nerves. Nearly an hour of purring along, with the conductor casually checking our tickets, and the warm glow of summer filling meadows and fields, means we all end up in a better mood. Mum nods off, while Arabella stares vacantly through the window, seeing nothing of the cows and sheep and fields that flash past her. I notice everything, from the yellow rape to the ball of dust that has collected underneath Arabella's seat, is coming loose with the motion of the train and

35

making the man opposite sneeze. A teenage girl stares at me across the gangway and smiles. It's a bit embarrassing and makes me fix my eyes on everything else for the next half hour. I don't look at her again, not until the end of the journey when she trips over the man's rucksack. I blush; she blushes. No-one else blushes or really notices, not even the man with the rucksack.

At Waterloo, Mum wakes with a start, leaps off the train and power walks us out of the station, onto the South Bank, over Hungerford Bridge, up the Embankment, across the Strand and into Trafalgar Square, leaving me struggling to keep up even in my flat, black shoes, and Arabella gasping for breath.

"Can't we take a taxi?" Arabella pleads.

"No need. We're here," Mum says, and there it is, the National Gallery, a huge monument of architectural splendour towering before us. London pounds around us, but once we've scaled the gallery steps and we're well inside, London is like a film I watch for a moment before switching channels and zooming into this world of vast, pictorial beauty. I'm so transfixed by the gallery, I hardly notice when Mum nudges me and says: "Where's Arry?"

Little does Mum know, but Arabella is incapable of getting lost in London. She's been here umpteen times on secret missions with boys and knows it like the back of her hand. So, her disappearance is much more likely to be deliberate than accidental. Still, twin duty kicks in and I start looking around for her and, surprise, surprise, only spot her practising her Italian on two glossy-haired Italian boys on the steps outside. The way she's flirting with them, you'd think she'd known them years!

"Mum wants you in there now," I say, pushing the door and pushing her in.

***

People don't talk much in art galleries, not in the exhibition rooms anyway. If they do, it's in hushed tones and muffled whispers, like pilgrims in a holy shrine. I think it must be something to do with the religious content of some of the paintings. They twist their heads into all sorts of positions, too. Course, Arabella thinks this is the dumbest thing on earth. She can't understand why people have to look at a painting sideways or upside down or turn the place into a morgue while they're doing it. But having studied art a bit, I kind of understand this sideways thing, twisting and tilting your head to get a different perspective on the picture, and I understand why Picasso's painting of *Weeping Woman*, that I'm looking at now, would make someone turn very quiet indeed. All those jagged shapes and symbols make the woman way too sad for words.

But I'm not especially sold on any of the paintings until I catch sight of one hanging in a space of its own in Room Two. It's a blue-green picture of a woman curled up naked on the floor with only her back half showing. Her head dips forward, resting on her folded arms, her dark hair is swept back loosely in a chignon, her legs are folded under her. I cannot see her face, making her seem distant, ethereal and infinitely mysterious, and yet her whole form speaks to me of sadness and peace and perturbation all at once.

I fight my way through the crowd to get to her, my heart racing. Up close, her beauty takes my breath away. She is called *Nu de Dos* and is all soft, sensual curves and warm, tranquil brush strokes; quite the opposite of *Weeping Woman*. Discovering her after all those jagged cubes is like entering a warm, flowing space, where I can move freely. I want to cry, she's so perfect. I gaze at her for several minutes, until the crowd pushes me on, and when I move away, something tears in my heart softly, like tissue.

In the shop afterwards, I buy a print of her and keep it hidden beneath the Monet tea towel I've bought for Mum, hoping I won't have to show it to anyone.

"Bought something nice?" Mum asks.

I hand her the tea towel and flip over the top of the bag. She smiles a knowing smile and doesn't ask anything more.

On the train home, Arabella amazes us by taking out this postcard she has bought of Picasso's *Lovers*. She says she *had* to have it. It's a picture of a dark-haired man with his arm around a woman who is dressed in yellow, green and white. The man looks adoringly at the woman, while the woman looks down shyly.

"He's just like Alex, isn't he?" she whispers in my ear.

I study the postcard hard, trying to figure out what she means. The man is gentle, handsome and kind, and if that's Alex, I'm the Queen of Sheba!

"Kind of," I say, not wanting to upset her.

She sighs quietly, closes her eyes and relaxes her grip on the postcard. It flutters through the air and flutters back, getting caught in the buttons of her black lacy top, where it hangs suspended. Her long, slender fingers skate over it and rest on its edges lightly, as if she's keeping it perfectly positioned, close to her heart.

Chapter Six

BOMBSHELL NUMBER FIVE… BRUNO IS BACK!

His green camper van is parked skew-whiff in our drive and he's skulking on the doorstep. His eyes dart everywhere, but mainly in the direction of Mrs Hodges's front garden, as if he's terrified any second she's going to take a potshot at him over the fence. Now he's rolling something around in his hands, which, from the bright yellow wrapping, looks suspiciously like a packet of jumbo bones for Sammy. Mum yelps when she spots him through the kitchen window and grips my arm.

"I'm going home," Arabella groans.

"You *are* home," I say, staring in stony amazement at Bruno.

From behind our front door, Sammy lets out a savage growl. For all his silky softness, he can be vicious when he wants to be, especially when it involves the mistreatment of his mistress and his favourite food bowl. If Bruno has any sense, he'll double back down the drive fast!

But miracles are funny things and two minutes later Bruno is well inside our house without a single nip to his ankles, and Sammy is securely locked in the kitchen. When I think about it, it wasn't a miracle at all. Mum just turned soft at the last minute (the minute Bruno purred sweet nothings at her through the letter box), and let Bruno in. Now they're in the sitting room trying to patch things up, and I'm hanging around outside, hoping any second Mum will pop her head round the door and announce Bruno is going *for good*.

I dare not interrupt them, so I steal into the back garden with Sammy, make a fake show of grooming him with his new wire brush, and then slip behind Mum's lilac bush, from where I have a bird's-eye view into the sitting room. Pretty weird, I know, to go spying on your mum and her ex, but I don't trust what's going on in there and have to find out.

Mum and Bruno are draped across the red Egyptian rug, half naked. By *half* naked, I mean Bruno has whipped off his shirt and sandals to reveal the hairiest chest and whitest feet I've ever seen, and Mum has taken off her shirt and tights and is playing Incy Wincy spider up his legs with her toes. Suddenly, Bruno produces a bunch of grapes from thin air, dangles it in front of Mum's lips, whips it away as Mum goes to bite one off, and they both roll around in hysterics. But far, *far* worse than this childish re-enactment of Antony and Cleo is the huge diamond crust flashing at me from the fourth finger of Mum's left hand, blinding me like a dart of intense sunlight. Knowing what it means, I sick up in the lilac bush.

Normally, I don't believe in hell and think it was probably a useful idea cooked up by some medieval despot to get money out of people and scare them into prayer. But if hell does exist, I think it must be something like this, with Mum and Bruno rolling around on that Egyptian rug, talking weddings. I think this must be hell of a kind because I can't actually imagine anything worse than it. Worse, I mean, than Bruno stepping into my real dad's shoes.

Sammy nudges me with his wet nose. *Arabella!* I've *got* to tell Arabella, otherwise I've broken our pact which states if anything mega serious happens in our family – i.e. *Mum getting engaged to Bruno* – we tell each other *instantly*.

After telling her, I wish I hadn't. She wails and moans and is more hysterical than Jane Austen's Marianne on a bad day. I have to stuff a cushion over her mouth to try to stop her noise, but it goes on and on, and in the end there's nothing for it but to smuggle her out of the house, and out of Mum and Bruno's hearing.

Her reaction to their engagement does seem a bit over the top, considering there are times when she actually seems to like Bruno, and I put this to her on the green outside.

"That doesn't mean I want him as my dad!" she sobs into the cushion.

"Me, neither," I say. "But I've been thinking about it, and he won't be, will he? He'll be…"

But before I can say exactly what Bruno will be, she's off again, and we look so peculiar on the edge of the green, with her wailing and weeping, and me trying to comfort her and shut her up at the same time, this guy cycles over to check we're OK. Then comes a stream of questions: "What's happened? Where do you live? Who are your parents? What can I do? Should I phone the police?"

It's a scary moment and takes some quick thinking from me to get us out of it. But I just about manage to, and soon we're walking in one direction, and the guy's pedalling away in another.

"Where are we going?" Arabella wails.

"To Alex's," I say, stunning myself. But we can't go home, and we can't stay on the green with everyone gawping, so we have to go to Alex's.

When we get there, Alex can only just stand up. Alex being Alex, and it being Friday night, I kind of expect this. He pushes the door wide, while I manoeuvre Arry into his black sitting room, with its black pictures, black window frames, black tables, black chairs, black shelves, black light shades and black just about everything else. All the black won't cheer Arry up much, but the shock of it might just curb her wailing.

Faz is there, lounging on the ripped black sofa, with Turpin, the ferret, running all over him, and there are a couple of other boys I don't know glued to a streaming of *The Mummy*. It's Alex's Boys' Night In and, drunk or not, he's pretty unimpressed to see us. When Arabella snuggles up to him, he stares coldly at her through a hazy glaze of lager and reluctantly plonks his arm across her shoulder, like a lump of lead piping.

A bit different from when he's out for all he can get, I think to myself.

41

"Arabella's had bad news," I say. "Don't upset her and *don't* get her pregnant!"

With that, I fly out of the black flat (never to return, I hope) and onto the first bus that comes along. I need some time alone to adjust to Bruno becoming a fully-fledged member of our family. The bus does the same circuit four times over, but I couldn't care less because when your life has just taken a major bulldozing, there's something quite comforting about staring at the same shops and pubs and office blocks and cafés over and over again. It kind of makes you feel safe inside.

"If you're not actually going anywhere, love, do you think you could get off at the next stop," the driver shouts. "You're taking up a seat for someone who needs it."

I can't see that I am. The bus isn't crowded, no-one is standing, and I've paid my fare like everyone else. But I obey him anyway because I'm too upset about Mum and Bruno and the engagement to get even more upset by having an argument with the bus driver. He drops me at the café, on the corner of Merton Street and, as it happens, a short walk from Shaun's house. Three minutes later, I'm outside Shaun's house, too scared to pull the bell, too unhappy to walk away without speaking to him. If only he'd come out, give me a big hug and say everything will be just fine, and I won't end up homeless just because I can't face Bruno across the Shreddies packet each morning. I can come live at his house instead.

I long for Shaun even more when I think of Mum with Bruno, and Arry with Alex, and me all on my own, and this feeling becomes so strong, suddenly, without meaning to, I'm pulling on the white ceramic knob, which is the Wilsons' front doorbell. Shaun opens the door and looks down at me. His feet are bare. His tanned, muscular thighs are hard and sinewy against his black cotton shorts. The late evening sun is casting ribbons of light over his face and he looks absolutely GORGEOUS! *So, so GORGEOUS*, it's all too much and I crash onto the gravel.

"That was some faint. Lucky I caught you," he murmurs in my ear.

The room I am in is all faded beauty; the chaise longue under me velvety and dusky pink. There are no sounds except for the distant, steady tick of a grandfather clock.

"How long have I been here?" I whisper.

"A couple of minutes. You collapsed outside. I had to carry you in."

"Where are your parents?"

"Out," he says, emphatically.

He passes me a tall crystal glass, full of glistening water, and steadies it while I take some sips. It feels cold in the room, freezing in fact, but then I realise it's not cold, it's me, and that I'm shivering, most probably from nerves or excitement, or both. I can't look at Shaun too much in case his *gorgeousness* makes me faint again, so I try focusing on something ugly, like the stoat head snarling at me from the top of Mrs Wilson's piano, but it's too horrible for words and masses of things swim before my eyes, like wreckage on a turbulent sea. Everything is like a dream: Mum's engagement to Bruno, Arry's wailing and moaning, Alex's nasty black flat, Shaun in his tight cotton shorts – a bad dream shifting to the best ever.

"Drink some more water," Shaun urges.

I take a gulp; it swishes around my mouth, warm and salty, like a tidal inlet.

"How do you feel now?"

"Fine," I lie, feeling utterly peculiar.

Shaun puts his arm around my shoulder and holds me close. It's a beautiful feeling of sinking into his warm, strong, sun-baked body. Then he turns me round, looks deeply into my eyes and runs his little finger over my bottom lip.

"You know I said my parents are out?"

"Yes," I say, hardly able to breathe.

"Well, they're not just out. They're out *all* evening."

"Oh," I murmur.

His breath is warm and syrupy, like sherbet lemons melting in the sun. His shiny black hair tickles my face. Then his mouth closes around mine and his tongue prises my lips open. It's the moment I've been waiting for – FOR FOUR WHOLE WEEKS – and I can't believe it's arrived! Half closing my eyes, I rotate my lips in the same direction as Shaun's. All I can hear is the tick, tick of the grandfather clock, and the fleshy grind of his lips against mine. All I can see, through my half-closed eyes, is Shaun's face pressed close to mine, and the thick drape of curtain he has pulled across the window to stop people looking in at us.

Shaun stops kissing me and starts again. This time his kiss goes on and on, and my lips get sorer and sorer, and my jaw starts to ache. I could do with some of that water, but I can't break off in case Shaun thinks I don't like him. *I mean, how often do I get a chance like this*? So, I push my lips round and round his, till it's like I'm back on that bus again, doing the same circuit four times over, stopping at the paper shop, the Square and Compass pub, the town council building, the café, popping my tongue in and out of Shaun's mouth with each stop.

The grandfather clock strikes eight p.m., Shaun's lips coil tightly around mine, his tongue speeds up in my mouth, his fingers sneak under my T-shirt and sidle up my bare stomach. I've always imagined Shaun's fingers would be cool and light and glide over my skin, like a skater. But they're damp and sticky and keep getting stuck on all my moles and lumpy bits, and caught up, like seaweed, in the soft, spongy area around my belly button. And just when things are feeling freer and smoother, and Shaun has managed to work his way out of my belly button and is en route to my left boob, I jump – right out of my skin! I can't help it. It just happens, and I'm worried sick then Shaun will take offence and go off me. But he doesn't. He stays his usual cool self and is just as cool ten seconds later when I tell him I need the toilet urgently, giving me a soppy dog look and urging me to come back *very soon*.

It takes me a while to locate the Wilsons' toilet, as this is a huge, rambling house with umpteen floors, and I haven't asked Shaun for directions. Two floors up and well inside the bathroom, I lean against the bolted door and stare at my reflection in the mirror. Waves of sweat are twirling and swirling around my face, which is as pink as a pomegranate. I don't use the toilet but flush it for effect, splash my face with cold water, wash my hands with the Imperial Leather soap in the soap dish and dry myself with the nice white linen towel hanging in the stainless steel hoop beside the basin.

Then I straighten my hair, take a deep breath and follow the winding staircase back down to Shaun.

Only, I don't go straight in. I hang back in the doorway, watching Shaun stretched out on the chaise longue, his eyes drifting over the crystal chandelier, and I discover there's something really special about just watching him like this and wish I could do it forever and didn't have to go back in. That's how I fell in love with him, you see: watching him at a distance, like a hero in a film, when he was on the football pitch or practising his sax in the music room all alone. Watching him, drinking in his beauty from afar, is a lot less scary than being bang up against him, like I was just now.

Back in the sitting room I stand beside the chaise longue, not really knowing what to do. But Shaun knows exactly. He pulls himself up, cups his hands around my face and draws me on top of him. "You're gorgeous," he says, as his hands creep over me, stroking all the bits he missed the first time, touching me in places I've *always* wanted him to touch me. But that's when I start to feel panicky. I try to push the feeling down and pretend it's not there, but it won't go away, so I say something I *know* will make Shaun stop.

"As gorgeous as Arabella?"

He stops and stares at me, like he's really confused. "Forget Arabella," he says, and before I can say another word, we're back on that bus again, snogging.

Who knows how far Shaun and I would have gone if Mrs Wilson hadn't walked in, but she does (right out of the blue) and the next thing I know Shaun's leaping off the chaise longue and I'm leaping with him, and we're trying to act like everything's normal – which isn't easy with the muscles in Shaun's neck red and throbbing like a bunch of boiled beetroots, and my face glowing like a high voltage fire. Mrs Wilson would have to be stupid not to twig. She smiles tactfully, asks if we've had a nice evening and offers to run me home – which I can't really refuse. And Shaun's dad, being a lofty professor of science and not too clever at chatting to teenage girls, just plain ignores me.

When I get home, things are different. The house reeks of Bruno's aftershave (a sure sign he's re-inhabited), Mum's bedroom door is shut tight for the first time in weeks, and Arabella has her ASLEEP – DO NOT DISTURB sign up, which means she's back from Alex's and is in no mood for talking. I shout out I'm home and take myself off to bed. All I want to do is forget everyone and everything: just rest my head on my pillow and pretend I'm no-one's twin, no-one's girlfriend and no-one's step-daughter-to-be. Just Sadie, in her own little bubble.

Chapter Seven

At two a.m. I wake with a jerk. The house is juddering and shuddering, as if in the grip of a violent earthquake. Groaning, I bury my head under my pillow, imagining weeks, months and years of Bruno squashing Mum to the width of a cucumber slice and driving me nuts with his vile sex sounds. In the end, I can't stand it any more. I search for my ear plugs, remember they're downstairs by the fish tank, reach for two bits of cotton wool to stuff in my ears instead and, just as I'm about to insert them, the noise stops.

I freeze, my right hand poised over my right earhole, waiting for Bruno to take off again. When he doesn't, I heave a huge sigh of relief, climb back into bed and drop into a deep, deep sleep, where I have this weird dream about a big, black poodle sniffing around a pretty King Charles spaniel and making her pregnant with ninety-nine puppies.

Next morning, I don't feel like going down. It takes me three tries to do it. Beneath the steaming coffee and stack of chocolate croissants lurks a deadly sense of impending doom. I can hear it in Mum's voice as she calls to me to tuck in. I can see it in Arabella's eyes as they narrow fearfully and scan the sitting room with icy mistrust. I can feel it, deep beneath my hunger pangs, in the bottom of my stomach.

There's no sign of Bruno anywhere, and no sign either that he's been evicted from the house; meaning he's keeping well out of the way until Mum has broken the news to us. I can tell, too, that however miserable Arabella is when Mum announces her engagement over breakfast, it will still be Arry, not me, who smiles graciously, mumbles congratulations and bends her head so low

Mum won't be able to see the truth in her eyes and, like the loyal and loving daughter she is, swallows virtually whole this repackaging of our life into the opposite of all that we have known and loved and trusted.

But then Arry isn't close to our real dad like I am. His full name is Justin Mark Preece and he runs a business called *Firefly*, taking artists under his wing and flogging their paintings. He's like a dad to all the budding Michelangelos who swan through his door – flattering them, telling them they paint like angels and persuading them he can make all their artistic dreams come true. Most of the time, he can, too. He's not just a flatterer – he's a brilliant businessman who can sell anything to anyone.

Most of what I know about art and literature, I owe to my dad. It was my dad who bought me Jane Eyre for my eleventh birthday and my dad who told me that in the best books there's both sadness and joy, and when you're going through a tough time there's always some character who has been there too and will bring you out the other side.

When Dad left us, I didn't know how to tell my friends. There are loads of friends I could have told, like Chloe and Ellie and Jake, who don't have dads themselves. But it was different for me because my dad didn't die, and he didn't leave us for a blonde bombshell, either. He didn't even go because he *wanted* to. In his words, he left because he *had* to. *Had* to be on his own, he said. Couldn't be a part of our family any more. Couldn't be with anyone any more. Had to be on his own, in his own space.

For hours I sat hunched up in his study, while he tried to explain, and I tried to understand. Mum was too upset to listen, so I tried to save her marriage for her. I tried but failed. Dad kept going on about needing to be on his own and how sorry he was and how he loved us deeply but couldn't help himself, and at the end of two hours of his talk my head felt like mashed potato. It was a relief to come out of that study and lose myself in Mum's warm, straightforward hug. But I suppose I did understand Dad a bit better after that. It's like the way I have to escape sometimes because Arry's being a pain or Bruno has cracked too many bad jokes. I *have* to get away from everyone and be on my own, the way Dad *had* to get away to his new life.

Dad and I are the same. We have the same *long-distance* gene, which makes us want to scarper when things come at us like a landslide. It's just that I go off to my room for a couple of hours, and Dad's gone off to his new life for good.

In a fantasy world, Mum would be with her man twenty-four hours a day. She has that *up close and personal* gene (oodles of it), so she couldn't understand Dad going at all; and he didn't help because right up to the moment he announced he was leaving, it seemed like *he* wanted to be with *us* twenty-four hours a day, too. For Mum, it must have been like going to bed with her husband and waking up with the bloke down the road. The one thing I can say about Bruno is, give or take the odd blip, he sticks around. He stands by Mum; he's there for her. I guess I should be grateful for that.

When Dad walked out, Mum phoned every friend in her mobile and then broke down sobbing. Arabella went out and spent two hundred pounds on clothes, *just like that*, and I took to my room. I couldn't eat; couldn't sleep. I couldn't even read the novels Dad said would get me through the tough times. No amount of wishing and hoping and praying could alter the pain I felt inside when I got up each morning and saw through my mesh curtains that the broad, blue outline of Dad's brand new Golf had receded to a blank, empty space. Nothing in the world could make up for the crinkled mound of Dad under the duvet suddenly becoming a smooth, flat plane of nothingness.

I never asked for these changes in my life, and every day they break my heart.

***

49

Twinhood is the ocean reaching into the shore. It is the dance of two seahorses circling each other, their tips touching. It is the sun backing down for the moon and the moon rising to reflect the sun's glory. So far, I haven't spoken to Arabella this morning. She's at the breakfast table, wearing her best smile ever, but her eyes give her away – they are like misty moons from all her crying last night. They fix on me, gigantic, watery orbs of expectation. Secretly, silently, she is asking me to carry her through the next half hour; she is speaking to me through the extrasensory cord that binds us, willing me to be the strength of the sun to her moon, the dominant seahorse in the dance, the strong, steady shore against her ocean.

Usually, she's the one who wants to be in charge, but today's different, and we are like a series of shifting and interchanging parts within one person. She swallows, I swallow. She drops her head mournfully, I arch mine defiantly. She shrinks, like a vanishing moon, I stand tall and erect by the window, pumping my strength to her. Never have we been so close nor understood each other so clearly. Never have we mirrored so acutely the similarities and differences that bind us.

Mum is tense when she comes into the breakfast room; the hairs on her arms are as stiff as porcupine bristles, and her hands are tightly clenched.

"There's something I want to tell you, girls."

Arabella reaches for the butter and slides her knife over it.

"Sadie, come and have something to eat," Mum says.

I edge towards the table and lower myself into the chair next to Arabella, and directly opposite Mum. I can hear Arabella breathing in short, sharp gasps, like a baby. Mum offers me a croissant and I take one. I can't stop staring at her clenched fist. From where I'm sitting, there's no sign of the diamond ring and I'm willing, willing, willing it not to be there.

"Arabella, Sadie, yesterday Bruno asked me to marry him… and

I accepted. I've spoken to Reverend Sommers, and he's agreed to marry us in St Julian's Church a year next September."

And that's it, really. The cat's out of the bag, there isn't so much as a squeak from Arabella and me, and Mum is smiling her broadest smile in years. Slowly but surely her fist unclenches, and there it is – the diamond crust – Big, Bombastic, Brunoish, booming at me from inside her left hand.

"Congratulations, Mum," Arabella mumbles, lowering her head and blowing Mum a huge kiss.

"Ditto," I say.

"Great ring," Arabella coos. "Bet it cost Bruno a fortune!"

"OK if I go now, Mum?" I ask.

"In a minute, Sadie. There's something I want to ask you both. It would really make my special day if you'd agree to be my bridesmaids."

My whole body turns to jelly. I can hardly look at Mum, let alone respond to her request. I stare down at my croissant, a crumbling mess on my plate and, without even meaning to, get up from my chair and push it hard under the table.

"Sadie?" Mum says, a terrible tremor pricking her voice. "You haven't finished your breakfast."

"I'm not hungry," I say, walking out.

Chapter Eight

I'm not proud of what I did; I'm dead ashamed of it, actually. But at the time, I couldn't help myself. It was the landslide thing, coming at me full pelt. I get Shaun to meet me early for the play auditions and crunch on his polo mints while I spill out everything, from Bruno and the jumbo bones, to walking out on Mum in a strop. He's so kind and understanding, I think how blessed I am to have him as my boyfriend, how amazing it is he has chosen *me* to be his girlfriend, and how I'd be a fool to make too much of my little panic at his house the other night.

Course, now Arabella is going to be a bridesmaid, she's overjoyed about the wedding, and just to prove this she's turned up at school and is bombarding me with talk of rings and dresses and veils and cakes and bells and confetti and champagne and canapés and kisses, and all the stuff that's supposed to make a wedding an unforgettably happy occasion. When she finally shuts up, I discover she's here to audition for the school play too, which is pretty weird considering she can't stand plays or Shakespeare.

The play is *A Midsummer Night's Dream* and anyone between eleven and sixteen, who can't think of anything better to do in the school holidays, can turn up to audition. Miss Ferris asks all thirty of us to hold hands in a circle and pretend we're the moon on midsummer night – just to get us in the mood, she says. What she's forgetting is that we're a bunch of school kids with sweaty palms and huge hang-ups about sex, so the last thing we want to do is touch each other. But then out come the typed sheets and name badges, and we either do what she says or exit.

I feel stupid wearing a name badge when most of the kids here know my name anyway. But then I notice Shaun polishing his and sliding it onto his jacket, and all my embarrassment seeps away. He can have this incredible effect, Shaun can, of making the stupidest thing seem the coolest. It's part of his natural style and sophistication.

"Sad," a voice pipes up. The boy next to me is staring at my badge, like he's never seen one like it, trying to figure out my name. Flinching, I look away.

"Sad… Sad," he keeps saying.

"I'M NOT SAD. I'M SADIE!" I bellow. "SADIE, NOT SAD. GOT IT? COS IF YOU HAVEN'T, YOU SHOULDN'T EVEN BE HERE!"

He turns bright red, shrinks into his chair and glues his eyes to his printed sheet, and I feel terrible. But I guess I'm severely stressed, what with weddings and bridesmaids, and Arabella being here when she shouldn't be and unable to take her eyes off Shaun, and me desperate to impress Miss Ferris because I'm desperate for the part of Titania and desperate for Shaun to get Oberon so we can be lovers on stage as well as off. So, when this boy says "Sad", I just flip!

Fortunately, Miss Ferris understands. "Don't worry," she says. "It's perfectly normal to be tense at the start of an audition. Sadie, why don't you launch us into things by reading Sonnet Eighteen at the bottom of sheet two?"

I unfold my printed sheet, glance at the sonnet, glance sublimely at Shaun and start reading:

> Shall I compare thee to a summer's day?
> Thou art more lovely and more temperate:
> Rough winds do shake the darling buds of May,
> And summer's lease hath all too short a date:
> Sometime too hot the eye of heaven shines,
> And often is his gold complexion dimm'd;
> And every fair from fair sometime declines,
> By chance, or nature's changing course, untrimm'd;

But thy eternal summer shall not fade,
Nor lose possession of that fair thou ow'st;
Nor shall death brag thou wander'st in his shade,
When in eternal lines to time thou grow'st;
So long as men can breathe, or eyes can see,
So long lives this, and this gives life to thee.

It's the perfect antidote to my rage and I wouldn't care if Shakespeare meant it for a giraffe – it's how I feel about Shaun, and reading it makes me feel a whole lot better. Arabella reads next, pretty well, I have to admit, considering the only poetry she knows are the twee little verses you get on Clinton birthday cards. Then Miss Ferris is looking at me again.

"Sheet four, halfway down. Sadie, you take Titania, and Miles, you take Oberon."

We launch into the "*ill met by moonlight*" speech, and even though my performance won't rock the world, I'm pretty confident it will get me a part (maybe even Titania), and if Shaun could get Oberon instead of whatsit next to me, all my dreams would come true.

"Now," Miss Ferris says, her eyes spinning round our circle like dice around a gambling wheel. "Shaun, you try Oberon, and Arabella, you try Titania."

My heart sinks. There's this loud snigger from somewhere in the circle as Shaun and Arabella rise together, and Shaun hangs back on the edge cos he's not sure what to do. Either he didn't expect Miss Ferris to audition him for such a big part or he's terrified of Arabella. Miss Ferris is getting twitchy: Shaun's acting like a lemon and she wants him centre stage, as Oberon should be.

"Move right in, Shaun," she shouts, her hands flapping everywhere. "The point about Oberon and Titania is that they're both strong characters and both want to be centre stage. They fancy each other like mad but have fallen out big time. The last thing Oberon would be doing is skulking in the shadows. Show us what you're made of, put some oomph into it, and remember you love her and hate her at the same time."

Right now, I can't see Arabella's face, but I can see Shaun's and it's like fire. He takes three huge strides into the circle and towers over Arabella, like a raging inferno. If he could take his eyes off her for two seconds (which he can't), he'd see me, his girlfriend, cheesed off in the chair behind her. But he's blanked me out. He's stopped being Shaun and become Oberon. Real life no longer exists for him. Sadie, his girlfriend, no longer exists for him. Fairy power has taken over.

Suddenly, he whips his jacket from his chair, slings it around his shoulders and starts stalking Arabella like a wild animal. *Ill met by moonlight, proud Titania*, he booms.

Arabella turns, flabbergasted. Never has Shaun been so macho and dominant.

What, jealous Oberon! Fairies skip hence; I have forsworn his bed and company.

Tarry, rash wanton: am not I thy lord? Shaun storms, swinging his jacket so hard it catches Arabella's left arm.

Then I must be thy lady... she whimpers.

The look they give each other then is enough to make me gag.

Afterwards, I feel rock bottom. I wait outside the girls' toilets for Miss Ferris to pin the results to the notice board and watch Shaun and Arry saunter off together and then saunter back with the rest of the drama lot. He's asking her something; she's shaking her head and splitting off from him, and now he's walking towards me, right up to me and straight past me, like I'm a ghost.

I feel like screaming, "Shaun! Shaun! Remember me? – SADIE! YOUR GIRLFRIEND!" but how stupid would that be! So, I just wander down the steps into the school garden and wait for Miss Ferris there. Guess who's beaten me to it? Only Arabella. She's over by the pond, staring up at the sky. Considering she's just spent the last hour flirting with my boyfriend, I don't exactly feel overjoyed to see her and nearly walk off. But NO, there are things I need to find out.

"What are you doing?" I ask, as she trails her foot through the grass, like a prima ballerina, and delicately positions it just where thick chunky strands wisp into tendrils of spring green.

"Just thinking. Where were you, Sadie? I looked everywhere for you."

Oh yeah, *everywhere*. I was only right under her nose!

"Weren't the auditions brilliant?" she says. "Miss Ferris is such a pro, and Shaun… wow… what an actor!"

She stares at the puffs of white floating above her, as if she's under some kind of spell.

"I just *had* to come into the garden; I *had* to lose myself in everything. It's so easy to forget how beautiful clouds are."

"Ummm," I mutter, thinking what a load of airy-fairy rubbish is coming out of her mouth. I mean, how do you forget how beautiful clouds are when you've never been interested in them in the first place?

"Sadie… can I borrow your copy of *A Midsummer Night's Dream* tonight? I want to read the rest of the play and find out what happens."

"On one condition," I say.

"What?"

"That if Miss Ferris offers you the part of Titania, you'll turn it down."

"Why?" she cries, like I've asked her to commit murder or something.

"That's why," I say.

"I can't, Sadie; not if she offers it."

"Yes, you can, if you *try*! I've made hundreds of sacrifices and done hundreds of favours for you, and the one time I ask you to do something for me, you refuse point blank. What kind of a twin is that?"

"I just can't!"

"Because of Shaun?"

"No, NOT because of Shaun. Because of ME, Sadie. I'm changing. Can't you see? I'm getting interested in things that bored me six months ago. I'm growing, learning, expanding, and it feels fantastic! It's like I've been shut in this tiny box with the lid screwed down and no air to breathe, and suddenly the sides expand and the lid pops open and the air rushes in, and I'm free!

I didn't know I had a creative side or that I could act till today, and I only turned up at the auditions because Alex says he fancies girls who experiment with new things. Doing those auditions made me express my feelings in other ways than slobbering all over Alex or whinging to you and Mum. If Miss Ferris offers me Titania, I can't say 'no' because it could be the only break I get."

"What, a break into the school pantomime, you mean?" I mutter sarcastically.

"No, into drama school, Sadie. I want to go to RADA."

"RADA? You're going to become a doctor, aren't you?"

"Don't be so sure about that. I'm not any more."

Just then I hear Miss Ferris's rubber heels twang the tarmacadam forecourt, and I get this horrible feeling my fate is about to be sealed. I charge off to the notice board and get there just as she's walking away.

"Great part for you there, Sadie. Hope you like it. Rehearsals start five p.m. prompt on Monday."

There are so many old notices about sports events and end-of-term concerts and school exchanges to France and Italy and sponsored walks and speech days, for a moment I can't even see the list. Then I spot Miss Ferris's spidery black loops, half tucked under a notice about the swimming gala, and I have to grip the board to steady myself. Surely, she hasn't given Titania to Arabella. Surely, she knows Shakespeare's about a lot more than just standing there, looking stunning. Trembling, I trace name after name, down line after line:

Theseus – Miles Thorne

Egeus – Daniel Wright

Lysander – Matthew Rivers

Demetrius – Charlie Brook

Hippolyta – Chrissie Wang

Hermia – Eloise Davies

Helena – Saskia Long

Oberon – Shaun Wilson

Titania – Arabella Preece

Puck – Amy Johnson

Bottom – Sadie Preece

"BOTTOM!" I scream. *There must be some mistake.* I know what it is: Miss Ferris has got me muddled up with Arabella. People are always doing that, even though we're not completely alike.

But then I remember the smirk on Miss Ferris's face: a jokey, half-embarrassed smirk, which said it all. She wants Arabella as the fairy queen and me as the *DONKEY*!

"Never mind," Shaun whispers, resting his chin on my shoulder and mumbling the list of names under his breath. "At least you'll get some laughs. Bottom's a great part; I wouldn't mind it myself."

"You can have it! Go tell Miss Ferris you're much better at comedy than I am and you're desperate to play Bottom. She likes you, Shaun. She'll do anything to keep you in the play. Just ask her," and I push him off towards Miss Ferris's office.

But Shaun doesn't want to because his eyes are already fixed on something else, i.e. the milky-white vision floating towards us like a dream, her hair scattered with loose beech leaves, her face adrift with excitement, and for two whole minutes he's utterly MESMERISED – till he remembers what the milky-white vision did to him outside the Odeon that time.

"Come on, Sadie. We've got *things* to do at my place," he snarls, and he grabs my arm and practically drags me out of school, without so much as a "Hi" or "Bye" to Arry.

***

Back at fifty-six Heathcote Drive later that evening, Mum's in the sitting room, cradling an old family photograph. From its bright gold frame, I recognise it as the one of the four of us on Weymouth beach: the sun's shining, Dad's chasing Mum with a slippery piece of seaweed, Mum's screaming and trying to dodge him, and Arry and I are chasing after them both, giggling our heads off. It was our last holiday before Dad walked out. I can't look at the photo too often because it makes me sad, and I can't understand why Mum has brought it out now.

She calls me over to the sofa. Her voice is strained, and her cheeks are sunken. She seems like a different person from this morning, when she announced her engagement over breakfast and couldn't stop smiling – and it's probably all my fault.

"Do you remember this day, Sadie?" she asks, pushing the photo under my nose.

Lowering my gaze to it is like being scorched by fire. I nod and look away quickly.

"You know, I wouldn't be marrying Bruno if our life were still like this. I wouldn't have booked the church or asked you to be my bridesmaid or done any of the things that give you so much pain. Your father was the love of my life and if he still loved me, none of this would be happening."

I clutch the wrinkled arm of the sofa and try to force back my tears. Mum's eyes are as dry as sandpits – she's done so much crying in the last three years, there's no more water to come out.

"But he's changed, Sadie, and you and I have to accept that. Bruno may not be your dad, but he's kind and thoughtful and wants *so much* to be your friend."

I stare a bit longer at the photo, its images of joy and light burning and blistering my pupils, and then I address Mum with this single question.

"What about Sammy?"

"What about him?" Mum replies, perplexed.

"Does Bruno want to be Sammy's friend, too?"

"Of course he does, Sadie."

"No, he doesn't. Look how roughly he treats him. Look what he did to his food bowl!"

Mum sighs heavily.

"Bruno was upset; he was worried about Arabella. He just lashed out at the first thing he saw, and it happened to be Sammy's food bowl." She pauses, like she's mulling over an additional thought. "But maybe you're right. Bruno's not used to dogs like we are, so it might be a good idea to keep Sammy downstairs for a few months, just while Bruno settles in."

So now Bruno's laying down the law about Sammy's domestic habits. Rule number one is that Sammy is not to climb onto beds any more or burst through bedroom doors unexpectedly, and once Bruno's an official member of our family, who knows what other rules we'll have to put up with. What Bruno doesn't get is that Sammy is no *ordinary* dog and my relationship with him is no *ordinary* relationship. He's Sammy the Noble, Sammy the Super-sensitive, Sammy the Supreme, and he means the WORLD to me. When Dad went off, who nursed me through my heartbreak with his constant love and attention? Only Sammy. And when, in a mad rage, I hurled my iPod at the bedroom wall, who stood there all calm and serene, his tail gently swishing, waiting for my pain to pass? Only Sammy. Banish Sammy and Bruno might as well banish me!

"Well, Sadie?" Mum's saying, her voice thick with anguish.

"I suppose so," I mumble.

She puts the photograph face down on the coffee table and opens her arms to me. I crawl into the narrow crevice of her body, feeling like I'm taking shelter in a piece of bark that might snap if I lean too heavily. Once, she was soft and easy to sink into, before all her weight dropped off. Now I have to shift around to get comfortable. I rest my head in the bony dip of her chest as she strokes my hair, and together we rock… rock… rock, like a battered coracle, far out on a gentle sea.

"I promise it will be all right, Sadie," she murmurs, rocking me.

I'm not sure I believe her, but just for now I feel very safe indeed.

Chapter Nine

So now I'm making my biggest effort yet to get on with Bruno. Which means:

1. Any present he buys me is graciously accepted with a smile and a peck on the cheek.
2. I keep Sammy under strict control, ensuring he doesn't slink upstairs to private bedrooms or plunge his wet muzzle into Bruno's Chinese takeaway.
3. I try hard to keep my lips zipped and my face like plastic when Bruno's being a pain.

In return, Bruno is sticking to his side of the bargain, which, unfortunately, doesn't mean an end to heaps of his smelly socks on the bathroom floor or tidemarks round the bath, but does mean taking the three of us for an Italian meal most Saturdays, footing the bill and going on endlessly about how he never wants to replace my dad and only wants to be my friend.

My heart would have to be stone not to be moved by his efforts. Still, I wish he wouldn't mention my dad *quite* so much and certainly not refer to him as the guy he *doesn't* want to replace. The more Bruno mentions Dad, the more upset I get, and the less chance there is of our new domestic arrangement working. Dad and Bruno just don't mix, not in my head, and not in real life, either. As long as Bruno's in one house, and my dad's at the opposite end of town in another, and I never have to see them together or feel the criss-cross emotions they stir up in me, I'll cope. But bring them together and it could be like a collision at Spaghetti Junction on a wet day.

On the whole, then, our house has pretty much returned to the normal calm of a near-normal family. Bruno and I are being nice to each other, Sammy's abiding by his new set of rules, Mum's in the second flush of love, and Arabella's out most nights, rehearsing Shakespeare (or secretly groping Alex). Not sure which.

About these rehearsals, I am as cool as a slice of melon fresh out of the fridge. Once I realised there was no way Arabella was going to turn down the part of Titania, I chilled. Seriously. I mean, just *what* can I do about it? Nothing – so there's no point in stressing. Anyway, there's a limit to what Arabella and Shaun can get up to under Miss Ferris's beady eye, and deep down I trust Shaun and have done ever since he said he wants me for myself and not because I'm Arry's twin.

I turned down the part of Bottom, though. Who, with any street cred, would want to neigh and bray and honk all night, while her twin sister plasters her with kisses and cuddles her like a boyfriend? Not me! Instead, I've opted to be wardrobe assistant – not the most exciting role in the world, but better any day than being a donkey. Part of my job is to accompany Arabella on a shopping trip for materials for her fairy costume, and she insists on John Lewis, Oxford Street, and nowhere else. After rifling through roll after roll of material, she finally pulls one of black fishnet and one of black satin off the shelf and dumps them in front of me.

"You can't wear that. It's way too sexy for Titania," I say.

"Titania *is* sexy, in case you haven't noticed. I've read the play and she's the sexiest character by miles."

"Ethereal, not sexy," I retort. "There *is* a difference, you know. No way would she have worn black net and satin. If you play her as a sexy bimbo, you miss conveying the empyreal world the fairies move in. You'll make her crude and obvious, and the whole meaning of fairyland will be lost."

"I don't see why," Arabella whines, fondling the black satin like it's her newly acquired pet panther. "Anyway, I don't want an argument about it. You see the play one way, Sadie, and I see it another. I'm having this material, full stop!"

In the end, it's Miss Ferris who puts a stop to the fishnet and satin. She wants Titania to reflect the forest and all that grows in it, which means *green* everything, minus the odd leaf and berry. Bottle green, in fact – Arabella's *least* favourite colour. Over the next four weeks, I spend hours cutting green and gold leaves from scraps of material, staining bits of cotton wool red with colouring for summer berries, drying twigs, collecting cones and sprigs of holly, and pinning the whole lot to a piece of bottle green muslin, which Arabella is *made* to wear over a bottle green leotard, like it or not.

When she sees her costume for the very first time, she bursts into tears and nearly pulls out of the play (nothing to do with me). She wants to be SEXY, she says, not SWAMPY, the green campaigner. What she fails to see, for all her whinging and cringing in front of the mirror, tugging at this leaf and that berry, is that this is the *best* she's ever looked! Green *really* suits her. It complements the blue of her eyes, like grass complements sky, and makes her hair shimmer like gold dust. Between us, Miss Ferris and I have managed to transform her from an above-average-looking teenage girl every boy wants to touch, to a visionary being the male sex would die for, and she's not even grateful!

"Perfect!" Miss Ferris exclaims. "A dryad of the woods. Exactly as I pictured you. Quite untouchable."

"Obviously," Arabella snorts, accidentally pricking her finger on a holly spike protruding from her chest.

"No, I mean rarefied, dreamlike; empowered yet remote. Against Oberon's maleness, you'll be a model of fecund femininity."

A glum shadow crosses Arabella's face. She's thinking of Alex in the front row, his face a dark, brooding storm cloud. Well, it's tough. If Alex is worth anything, he'll want her twigs, sprigs and all. What else is love about?

"You'll do it then?" Shaun says. "Sure you don't mind?"

"Course I don't mind," I say. For Shaun, I'd do almost anything.

"She's OK, you know. It's just that my German's useless, and Mum and Dad don't seem to understand that when I take her places, she gets bored, and I can't leave her at home, so…"

"I'll do it!" I say, pressing my lips to his in front of our friends. Our snogging is pretty good these days. It's getting more advanced by the week, and we've even graduated to doing it in public places, like here in the middle of town.

"You're brill, Sadie," he says, pulling away from me shyly. "Her name is Anneliese and she's over there in Pizza Palace. All you have to do is go introduce yourself."

Easier said than done, I think. I take my time crossing the road because this is a nerve-racking assignment my boyfriend has just given me. For one thing, I don't speak German; for another, I've never *been* to Germany; and, for a third, I've never had to look after a complete stranger before, who also happens to be my boyfriend's German Facebook mate.

Inside Pizza Palace I know instantly which girl is Anneliese because she's the only one asking for German cheese on her pizza. She's tall and bronzed (real, not fake), with loads of thick reddish hair tumbling down her back, and when she speaks to the waiter she keeps saying "so", which sounds like "zo". I can tell already that her English is ten times better than anyone's in my school, making me think she's either secretly English (and only pretending to be German), or she's German and sleeps with an English dictionary under her pillow. I stride over to her table (the *only* way to conquer my nerves), plonk myself down and say: "Hi, I'm Sadie, Shaun's girlfriend, and guess what? I've come to look after you."

Something about my voice must be truly *hideous* because she sinks about ten inches under the table and gives me this frozen, terrified smile: the kind you'd give a big, hairy monster you *have* to be nice to, in case it gobbles you up. I won't kid you that the next few minutes between the arrival of the hairy monster (i.e. me) and the arrival of the pizza are easy – they're not! I have to grope around for things to say and all I come up with are a load of ums and ahs and ers and urs and oohs, and sometimes not even an um, ah, er, ur or ooh; just a long, horrible silence, which makes *me* want to slide under the table too.

But I ride this sticky patch and before I know it the pizza's arrived, and Anneliese is staring at it, gobsmacked, saying it's way too big for her to eat on her own, and I'm saying "I'll help you" (cos I'm ravenous), and either because the stuff sprinkled on top is pure *magic* or just crammed with a load of E numbers, suddenly Anneliese is jabbering non-stop, and I'm eating and jabbering non-stop too, and there's nothing any more to worry about.

I discover her mum is fifty-five, her dad is fifty-six, her sister, Heidi, is a wild and wacky eight, and her pet gerbils, Ricky and Peter, are one and two months and minuscule. She discovers my mum is forty-nine, my dad is fifty-one, my twin sister, Arry, is a wild and wacky sixteen, and my Golden Retriever, Sammy, is six and MAGNIFICENT. Then she says she loves tea and wouldn't it be nice to go somewhere quaint and British to drink some, and I have this brainwave to take her to Molly's Teashop, where the waitresses flounce around in frilly white aprons, and the manager stands over them like a stern headmaster, and the outside of the shop is like a wooden zebra crossing and the inside like a country cottage (only *much* nicer than Alex's), and so we go. First, it's my smartest move of the day (cos Anneliese loves it) and then it's my dumbest (cos I can't get her out of there). She drains the teashop dry, fiddles with all the stuff on the display unit and can't make up her mind what to buy.

"Er, I think they want to close now, Anneliese," I say, trying to drop an enormous hint without sounding too rude. It works, because suddenly she's buying up all this stuff and we're out of there.

66

"Zo, Sadie, now that we have all this tea, we will go to Shaun's house to brew it."

More tea, I groan inwardly. Why can't it be Coke or orange juice or just plain water? *More* tea, at Shaun's, when he won't even be there. It's kind of hard to swallow.

Anyway, I nod politely and escort her to Lime Tree Avenue, where going into Shaun's without him is like going in naked. Anneliese is laid-back about it, though. She says Mrs Wilson doesn't mind who comes and goes, and Shaun definitely doesn't, and Professor Wilson, if he ever noticed people, wouldn't mind, either. It's important, she says, to treat the place you're visiting as home and the people in it as your family, otherwise you get homesick for your *real* home and your *real* family, and offend your hosts by boarding the first plane back. I kind of see her point. I see, too, that she's a girl who knows what she wants and where she's going – which is refreshing for someone like me, who's only just waking up to that kind of stuff.

"Zo, tea, tea, tea, tea, tea, tea, tea, tea, tea!" Anneliese exclaims, as she unwraps all nine packets of Assam, Darjeeling, English Breakfast, Earl Grey, Lapsang Souchong, rose, orange, ginger and peppermint, and starts brewing them. Within minutes, Mrs Wilson's kitchen is looking and smelling like a chemistry experiment gone wrong, and I'm groping my way through all the steam and fumes, terrified of accidentally knocking noses with the professor.

Anneliese concocts this game, where she brews a mug of tea, hands it to me, I sniff and sip it, give it marks out of ten and hand it back to her. Mostly, I give it a two or a three cos it's not very nice or, if I'm feeling generous, a five or a six – unless it's really disgusting, in which case I give zero out of ten. But when the peppermint tea comes my way, something amazing happens! I take a huge sniff and a gulp and instantly my mood lifts and my stomach grows as calm as the Sea of Galilee, which means I award a cracking ten out of ten, and Anneliese leaps around the kitchen ecstatically.

"A gift for you, Sadie, for looking after me today," she says, handing me the packet of peppermint tea. "Otherwise, I would have been zo, zo bored, and I have not been bored at all! Zo, now we go and meet Shaun."

"Yes, now we go and meet Shaun," I say.

***

The second time I look after Anneliese, it's cold and wet. We're in Molly's Tea Shop, sipping lemon tea (just for a change), and Anneliese isn't happy. She slumps at the table in jeans and a brown T-shirt and acts like she doesn't want to be here at all. I don't like to ask where she'd rather be, but I suspect it's back in Munich with her mum, dad, sister Heidi, and pet gerbils, Ricky and Peter.

Tugging at strands of her long, red hair, which today is piled high in lush chunks on top of her head and only just held together by an orange slide, she stares wistfully at the other tea drinkers, then mournfully at this woman munching on her shortbread, and it's at this moment it dawns on me I'm dealing with one seriously moody teenager.

"So, what are German boys like?" I ask, trying my best to drag her out of her mood.

I've told her everything I know about British boys (which is basically Shaun, Shaun and Shaun) and I want to find out about boys in Germany, with a view perhaps to one day having a mysterious cosmopolitan affair – if Shaun and I don't work out, I mean.

"Ah, boys in Germany, they are all the same," she says, waving her hand through the air dismissively and cutting our conversation dead.

This can only mean one of two things: either Anneliese is bored by all the German boys she knows and is biding her time until she can move on to German men, or she's just been jilted by her boyfriend (maybe even at the airport), is hurting badly and doesn't want to talk about it. An imaginary Kurt springs into my head: "Bye, Anneliese, have a great time, Anneliese… sorry, won't see you when you're back cos we're over, finished, kaput."

Judging by the lost, sad look in her eyes, I guess it's the second thing, and I mustn't ask too many questions. So, we just sit here, sipping our tea and making patterns in the sugar with our spoons, our eyes meeting every so often in the kind of smile girls give when they don't know each other very well, waiting for afternoon to nudge into evening, and Shaun to show up.

Once, during the course of the afternoon, Anneliese's mood changes so rapidly and she gets so excited, I think she's about to blurt out something really private about herself. But then her expression grows serious, her lips close around her words, she yanks out her slide and great, red chunks of hair come crashing down around her shoulders in an avalanche of secrets never to be revealed.

That's when I decide she's not just sad, moody and hard to read, but interesting and different from anyone I've ever known and reminds me of one of those Pre-Raphaelite models Rossetti and Burne-Jones used to paint. The more I think about this, the more true it seems, and the more my glance and smile become a smile and a stare, until I'm convinced she's visiting from another time, another world, another place.

She glances at me for longer then, her smile warming and deepening, her mood lifting and shifting to something much brighter, as if she senses I'm not thinking about boys and boyfriends any more, but about *her* – the way she looks, the way she is – and I have to turn away because I can't take the incredible light that has just come into her eyes.

Chapter Ten

Someone's following us. A man, in the evenings, down alleyways, outside shops, *everywhere* it seems, and he's spooking me. As soon as I turn to see who he is, he dodges behind a lamp post or shoots into a doorway or zooms off so fast in his car I can't get his number plate. I haven't said anything to Anneliese because I don't want to freak her out in a strange country, but she must know something's up because we'll be strolling along quite normally when suddenly my breathing quickens and I'm shoving her into the nearest shop.

I'm about to tell Mum when there's something else. It's a foggy evening in early September, and I'm looking after Anneliese again. We've just bought a bag of chips and are eating them as we walk along because it's after five-thirty and there's nowhere much to go. In the distance, I hear the roar of a car engine getting louder and louder. I turn and see this black car speeding towards us at top speed. I hurl myself against Anneliese, in case it's a madman trying to kill us, and the car screeches to a halt. The driver winds down his window, pulls off his baseball cap and sticks his head out. There's a strong smell of putty, and a set of crooked yellow teeth poking out at me.

"FAZ! What the hell are you doing? You nearly killed us!" I scream.

Anneliese is rigid with fear. I have to prop her against the wall to stop her from toppling over like a lopped tree trunk.

"Sorry," Faz mutters, smirking sheepishly. He pushes on his cap and then pulls it off, and just sits there, gawping at us.

"It's not funny. You've been following us for days. I was about to go to the police. I still might!"

"No harm meant, Sadie. But I could hardly knock you up – your folks might not have liked it. I've got something to tell you."

"I'm not interested," I say, shaking with shock. It's cold out here, there's fog on my chips and I just want to go home.

"Ten minutes, Sadie," Faz pleads. "Ten minutes in the back of my car, warming up with the heater and some music, eating your chips and chatting."

I've only met Faz twice in my life and both times he struck me as peculiar. So, it's not surprising I don't want to get into his smelly car, or share my chips with him, or listen to his music, even if he is the best friend of my future brother-in-law and one day I'll have to play bridesmaid to his best man.

"No!" I exclaim.

"*Please*, Sadie. You'll thank me when you know."

In the end, I give in, because I'm just too nosy not to. I arrange Anneliese in the back seat and sit next to her, while Turpin the ferret scampers everywhere.

"You could be done for having a loose animal in the car," I say. "It's a distraction. It could cause an accident, and you could lose your licence!"

"You know, that's just what I like about you, Sadie – the way you always tell it as it is. It's kind of cute."

I shut up then because something tender has crept into Faz's voice, and I'm used to Faz the Twerp or Faz the Sarcastic.

"Say what you have to say, Faz, and we can all go home."

"Well, it's not quite as simple as that, Sadie. It kind of involves going somewhere," he mutters, stretching out his hand, snapping up my fattest chip and offering it to the ferret, which sinks its claws into it, "and showing you something. Otherwise, what I tell you and what you choose to believe won't add up."

"Stop playing games with me, Faz, and just tell me what it is."

"All right then," he says, with a sigh so enormous it knocks me back against the car seat. "It's about Alex… and your twin."

I know then I have to go with Faz, even if he's lying, otherwise I won't be doing my duty to Arabella. All the way to the Jolly Frog pub, Faz drives extra slowly, like Anneliese and I are a couple of eggs he's scared of cracking. He backs into the pub car park, gets out and opens the door for me.

"Over there," he says, jerking his head towards the back entrance of the pub. "No need to go in. You can see it all from the back door."

"Who am I looking for?" I ask.

"You'll see."

At first, there's just a blur of colour: the greens, blacks, reds and blues of people's clothes, and the thick, murky swell of their bodies against the bar. But then Faz puts his hands on my shoulders and steadily turns me in the right direction.

"There, see, the green pool table in the corner."

For a moment, I don't recognise Alex because he's not in his customary black, his hair has been cropped and he has his back to me. But when he turns and takes up his cue, the smug smile he gives his mate pierces me with its certainty. That's Alex all right – no mistaking. He plays a couple of shots, thrusts the cue into the air triumphantly, plays another shot and misses, and sinks down onto the bench, right next to this girl, who looks just like him. For all I know, she could be his cousin or his long-lost sister or the twin no-one knew he had. But after watching them for several minutes, I realise you don't touch your cousin or your long-lost sister or your twin like *that*!

"See them?" Faz asks.

"I see them," I say, a chilling numbness stealing through my whole body.

Back in the car, I let rip.

"Why the hell did you have to tell me, Faz? Alex is YOUR friend. Arabella is MY twin. Why did you have to dump it on me? It's not fair. You should *never, ever* have brought me here!"

"Thought I was doing the decent thing, didn't I," he mumbles, guiltily. "Whatever you think, Sadie, I'm actually doing Arry a favour. Alex is stringing her along something rotten; using her

72

for his own warped pleasure when Melissa is out of town. It only seemed fair you should know."

"But Alex is your *best friend*, and you've just split on him! If he finds out, he'll either beat you up or dump you."

"Second best. My best is Ferdy, up in Newcastle."

"Well, I still don't get it. Why drag me into it? Why not go straight to Arabella?"

"It sounds better coming from a twin; softens the blow a bit," Faz mumbles.

"Why bother to say anything, though?"

This time he doesn't reply – just gives me this long, puppyish look through his slate-grey eyes, and I think I know the reason.

"If I hadn't told you, Sadie, you'd have found out anyway in time. I just set the ball rolling. Think of it that way."

The ferret gnaws my little finger, and Anneliese tries her best to comfort me, but I just want to get away from here; curl up somewhere on my own with my bag of chips and pretend none of this happened, that I saw nothing, *nothing at all* in the Jolly Frog.

"I had to show you, Sadie, cos there's no way you'd have believed me otherwise."

"And now I have to tell Arabella. Alex is GOD to her!"

"There's more, I'm afraid," Faz murmurs, swallowing hard. "Melissa's pregnant. The two of them are getting married next summer. Baby's due in March."

***

This is the question: is it better to tell the twin you love the truth and hurt her terribly, or keep the truth from her and let her live a terrible lie? It's one of those agonising life decisions I shouldn't be faced with at sixteen. But life being as it is, and Faz being as he is, I am.

I don't know the answer. All I know is it's no fun being saddled with this problem when everyone else is riding free of it. Like the time when I get home from school, my problem weighing on me like King Kong, and everyone's happy and relaxed. Mum's putting the finishing touches on Bruno's fiftieth birthday cake, Sammy's snoozing by the fire, his nose twitching with pleasure, Arabella's curled up in the armchair, leafing through Mum's bridal magazine (and secretly storing up designs and colours for her own wedding) and Bruno's singing in the bathroom. It's a merry picture, which only makes me feel ten times worse.

I force a smile, greet everyone as per normal and don't breathe a word about what I saw in the Jolly Frog six nights earlier. Nor do I breathe a word to Arry when she's alone, cleaning her teeth or undressing for bed. But somehow, not breathing a word doesn't solve my problem; it just shelves it.

In bed at night, I think about the only two people in the world who know what I'm going through: Faz and Anneliese. Obviously, I can't talk to Faz, in case he gets the wrong idea and hots up on me, and anyway he's disappeared off the face of the earth. As for Anneliese... well, next evening I try it out on her.

"Anneliese, you know what I saw that night in the Jolly Frog...?"

Anneliese listens as I pour out my heart, her deep brown eyes focusing intently on me, as if I'm the most important person in the world, and my problem the only one worth considering. I learn quickly then that she has one of those soft, elastic hearts, which expands the more you press on it. Not like some girls I know, whose hearts get harder and narrower each time I tell them something serious. If Anneliese takes some getting to know, at least beneath her mixed moods and brooding silences lies a warm, loving person.

Once she's heard me out, she's ready for action.

"Zo, Sadie, you must go and tell your twin now. I shall come with you and wait outside your house. It is not good to live a lie, not for you and not for her. Once she knows the truth, it will hurt like hell, but one day she will wake up and the pain will have gone. Better to have a short, sharp shock than a long, dreary ache that goes on and on."

Deep down, I know Anneliese is right. I've probably always known, but for some reason I needed her to tell me. As I finish off my slice of Victoria sponge in Molly's, I imagine this to be the last bit of sweetness I will know for a while. We pick up our coats and head east through town against the evening rush of commuters, up Barker Street, over the old, rusting suspension bridge, which tries to push us back with each step we take, and onwards to my house.

A savage wind cuts into us, churning up bottles, cartons, old newspapers, stray bits of wood and straw from gutters and drains, and I can hardly see for all the rubbish coming at me. But nothing is as bad as my dread of what lies ahead. If I didn't have Anneliese by my side, I'd turn and run. The strength of her presence keeps me going; that, and the warm, encouraging way she catches hold of my hand and squeezes it, saying, "Don't be afraid, my friend. I am here. I am with you."

The house is steeped in darkness, except for a solitary circle of pink light protruding from the side wall: Arabella's light. My stomach turns over. All the way here, I've been praying Arabella would be out with Alex and I'd be able to put off telling her. Now, as I gaze up at her window, it seems like something larger and more forceful than my own little will has brought me to this point, and I know I have to go through with it.

"She's in," I say.

"Yes. Be strong, Sadie. I will wait for you here," Anneliese replies, squeezing my hand for the last time.

I rummage in my bag for my door key, gripping it so hard it breaks my skin. Then I enter the house as quietly as an intruder. Arabella's bedroom door is closed. For a moment, I just stand outside it, too scared to do anything. When I tap it and enter, she shrieks.

"God, I didn't hear you come in. Why are all the lights off? Where are Mum and Bruno anyway? They've been out hours!"

"I don't know," I say. Mum and Bruno are the last people on

my mind. It's Arabella and Alex I can't get off it. Like a reluctant trespasser, I hover awkwardly by her door, before blurting out:

"There's something I've got to tell you, Arry."

"What?" she says, eyeing me curiously.

She is stretched out on her satin bedspread, exactly as I hoped she wouldn't be – freshly showered, wrapped in her white fluffy bathrobe, her face free of all traces of make-up; as pure and untouched as a princess in her chamber. I wish with all my heart she were dressed for a party, heavily made up with loads of mascara, eyeliner, foundation and blusher, and that she looked like an adult, with a hard, adult shell to protect her.

"Good, bad, red hot or boring? Come on, Sadie, I'm desperate to know," she says, but already I can hear the fear in her voice.

"Are you *sure* you want to know, Arry?" I ask, staring down at the carpet.

"Course I do," she murmurs.

"OK, then. Alex is seeing someone else. She's called Melissa. She's pregnant with his kid and they're getting married next summer."

I don't know what to expect – hysterics probably: that she'll sob into her bedspread or scream *proof? proof? proof?* at me or charge out into the night after Alex. But she doesn't do any of these things. She doesn't even cry. She just remains motionless on her bed, as limp as a newborn lamb, her milk-white legs dangling over its sides, the huge round birthmark on her left thigh thrusting out at me, her eyes drifting, drifting everywhere. I've never wanted to hug her so much in my whole life, and never felt more strongly that this would be the worst thing I could possibly do. So, I just keep standing here.

"How do you know?" she asks, after a minute or two.

"Faz told me."

"How do you know he's telling the truth? He's jealous of Alex and me. He could be trying to split us up."

"He took me to the pub. They were together, Arry. *Really* together. I saw them."

She gives me a glance which is so full of pain, I begin to understand why her eyes can't settle on anything, why they have to drift and drift. Suddenly, it's all too much for me: her sadness bloating the room; her anger with Alex; all the questions she's desperate to ask me, poised on the tip of her tongue. I don't want her to ask me anything. I don't want to be made to describe what I saw that night – what Melissa looked like and what she was wearing; what Alex was doing to her, and she to him. I want to forget it all, and I want Arry to forget, too.

"Is she… *very* pretty?" she murmurs.

"Nope. Not half as pretty as you. He's seriously dumb."

"Oh," she says, closing her fingers around a satin square. "I think I want to be on my own now, Sadie."

"OK then," I say, turning towards the door and instantly turning back again.

"I *was* right to tell you though, wasn't I, Arry?"

"Course," she whimpers, and she turns over, places her cheek flat against the satin bedspread and shuts me out.

In total darkness, I fumble down the stairs into the dining room and crawl under the table and across to the small, square oak cabinet in the corner of the room. It's Bruno's drinks cabinet, and I am forbidden to open it. I reach for the key hanging on a piece of string behind the cabinet and press it into the lock. The door springs open and a small light bulb comes on, illuminating rows and rows of glass bottles. I dip my hands behind the first row and close them around the fat brandy bottle Bruno brings out on Friday nights. I unscrew the cap and take an enormous swig. It misses my mouth and runs down my chin onto my jumper. Steadying the bottle, I take another swig, and this time the liquid goes straight into my mouth, down my throat and into my stomach, where it warms and burns like fire.

Quickly, I re-screw the cap, wipe the bottle dry with my sleeve, put it back on the shelf, snap shut the cabinet door, hang up the key and crawl back under the table, thinking… I don't know what I'm thinking: that swigging that brandy was the dumbest thing to do; that I feel more shaky, not less; that Alex is some dark force driving me to do stupid things, and making my twin the unhappiest girl on earth.

Then I remember Anneliese waiting outside for me. I clamber from under the table and peer through the darkened window. There she is, waiting patiently, her thick chunks of hair gleaming red and gold in the lamp light. Within seconds, I've left behind the morbid atmosphere of the house and am next to her on the pavement.

Chapter Eleven

When Arabella and Alex finally split, Arabella doesn't shed a single tear. Instead, she turns sullen and picks at her food (which worries Mum to death). One night, soon after their split, she confides to me that when she and Alex were together the whole world lit up like a beacon, and now he's gone a shadow covers everything. As far as I'm concerned, Alex *was* the shadow but try telling her that.

So, for now, Arabella minus Alex = Arabella lost, lonely and hurt. She's started to use Shaun and me as an oversized comfort blanket – a bit too regularly for my liking. I mean, I know she's my twin and I have to look out for her, but three's a crowd sometimes. When Anneliese joins us and three becomes four, Arabella complains she doesn't get her, and why should she be lumped with someone she doesn't get while Shaun and I are getting stuck into each other behind the wheelie bins? But this is just another of Arry's self-made myths. Shaun and I *never* get stuck in when she's around. For one thing, we never get the chance (we're hardly free of her for more than two minutes). For another, I'm not her!

"No-one's making you come out with us," I say. "You can stay home alone, for all I care."

Fat chance of that, though. Home alone makes Arabella jittery. Being boy-less makes her jittery. Having nothing to do makes her jittery. The only solution to her triple dose of the jitters is to cling to Shaun and me for dear life and bag the first boy who comes along. Which she tries to do but fails. Not like Arry, and not like boys with Arry, either, but that's the way the cookie's crumbling for her at the moment.

The third time she tries to get off with this boy called Brad, by practically flinging herself on top of him in Pizza Palace, Shaun goes crazy. He marches her out of the restaurant and into the town square, where he delivers this lecture in the freezing cold on what she *should* and *shouldn't* do in public.

"Stop being Oberon, Shaun!" Arabella proclaims haughtily. "You're *not* my lover and you're *not* my dad, either, so stop trying to be!"

A faint flicker of regret crosses Shaun's face but passes as swiftly as the fog around our heads, and before we know it Arry's antics are forgotten, until next time – two days later.

I suppose if I were strong enough or hard enough or selfish enough or just plain nasty enough, I'd tell Arry where to go. But I haven't the heart. She's already been hurt by Alex, so she can't be hurt by Shaun and me, too. All the time, though, a small, quiet voice is whispering in my ear: "Take care, Sadie. Take very good care."

The voice is my dad's and hearing it after a month of no contact with him is *beautiful*. On Saturday the third of October, he phones to invite me to ten Orchard Close, his brand new house in a cul-de-sac on the south side of town. Nerves sprout like triffids in my stomach, and my fingernails replace my midday meal. I don't know why I'm so scared. After all, he's only my dad. But a million worrying thoughts fill my head. Will he look different? Will he act differently? Will he have a girlfriend stashed away in the loft? Will he still have the silver cufflinks I bought him last Christmas or have chucked them out with the Christmas dinner scraps? Will he rave about his new life? Will he mention Mum? Will he *ever* change his mind and come home to us, before it's completely too late?

When I see ten Orchard Close for the first time, I nearly break my golden rule never, ever to cry in public. It's just like our house, only smaller – a mini version of home. There are red and gold strands of creeper trailing the brown brick walls, just like at home. There's an oblong dugout on the front lawn that will soon be a pond, just like at home. There's a box hedge skirting the front path, and even a lilac bush, just like at home.

Dad opens the front door and gives me a huge smile. He's wearing black jeans and a turquoise Boden shirt and looks fantastic. I can hear his favourite Van Morrison track playing in the background, smell his aramis aftershave as he leans to kiss me, see all his Constables, Whistlers and Monets stacked up against the hall wall, feel oodles of love pouring out of him, just for me, only for me, and I hurl myself into his arms, sobbing.

We collapse on the bottom stair. He cries too – not like me with loud, clucking gulps, but quietly, gently, like I always imagined he would cry. He cries and holds me, strokes my hair, kisses away my fringe and squeezes my arms till they hurt. Gulping, I beg him to come home to us. I don't care if it's wrong to ask. It's all I want.

He pulls me closer and binds his arms around me, so I can hardly breathe. My face is tight against his chest.

"Please, Dad, please. It's not the same with Bruno. He plays heavy metal and makes vile sex sounds in the middle of the night. He's the *opposite* of you. Please, Dad! I miss you. Arry misses you. Sammy misses you. *Please, please come home!*"

But I'm not six any more, begging for my third bedtime story. I'm sixteen and begging for something much bigger. Something Dad can't just pull off a bookshelf. Something I know in my heart he won't say 'yes' to, no matter how much I gulp my way there. Ever so gently, he prises me from his chest, takes out his large cotton handkerchief and presses it into my hand. I clutch it, feeling I'll never let it go. He runs his fingers through my hair and cups my face with his hands. His cornflower blue eyes are full of sorrow.

"You know I can't come back, Sadie. Things have changed. Your mum's getting married. I'm living here. We all have a new life now. We've all started again. It's important that you do too, otherwise you'll be left behind, and I can't have that happening to my little Sadie. From what I've heard, Bruno's not such a bad guy. He's fair and kind – probably kinder than me in many ways. You mustn't hate him just because he's different from me. If he were the same, it would be even harder."

I blow my nose on his handkerchief and try to concentrate on the coloured flecks of light roaming the hall walls. Once, I respected my dad for his honesty: the way he always spoke the truth, never lied, and always gave Arry and me a blasting if we lied. But right now, I think his honesty is the thing I hate most, and just for once I wish he could be a really big liar who makes up great, whopping stories about how he misses us dreadfully, is desperate to come home and is popping upstairs right now to pack his bag. I wish he were really good at pretending because then he'd never have gone in the first place.

His bony knee digs into my thigh. "I love you, Sadie. I want the very best for you – always."

He's still my dad, still loves me, still wears the same clothes and has the same pictures lying round the place and the same music playing. But something has changed, completely and forever, and I know that now. Here, in his new house, his arms and legs move more freely, and the deadness has gone from his eyes. There's a freedom in his face I've never seen before. I can't pretend it's not there because, like him, I'm no good at pretending.

"Come on, love. I'll make you a cup of tea," he says, helping me up and leading me into the kitchen. "How about you pick a DVD, and we watch it together, or we can stream one of your favourite films?"

There's this purple scarf hanging on the kitchen chair: a beautiful silk one, delicately embroidered with tiny pearls. When Dad's filling the kettle, I give it a secret sniff. As I expect, it smells of perfume.

"Whose scarf?" I ask.

Dad turns and looks at it as if he hasn't even noticed it's there.

"Oh, it must be Kathy's. She popped over the other day. You know, Kathy Walters, old family friend, *very* happily married, lives in London with kids Becky and George."

"Yes," I say, feeling embarrassed.

"I don't have a girlfriend, Sadie, if that's what you're thinking.

All this, my move, my new house, they're not about another woman. Remember?"

"Yes," I say again. How could I ever forget when he spent hours drumming it into me in his study.

But I want to scream and shout, lash out with my fists, say I wish it *were* about another woman; wish he'd slept with hundreds of women and left Mum for each of them, instead of leaving for no real reason at all, just so he can have a nice time in his brand new house, swinging his legs like a kid. His reasons for going are *dumb*, *stupid*, the most rubbish reasons anyone's ever come up with. They don't make sense. They're like flimsy flakes of snow that melt as soon as you put your hands on them.

"I can't watch a film. Mum's expecting me in an hour."

"That's a shame. Next time, maybe," he says sadly.

After tea, we kiss goodbye on the doorstep and say we love each other, which I guess is true. He tells me to visit any time, all the time, treat his house like home. Halfway down the garden path, something makes me stop and look round at him.

"Any message for Mum?" I call back.

He steps into the garden in his bare feet. For a moment, I think he's coming down the path after me. "Tell her…" and then he stops. "No, no message," he says.

I don't even remember the journey home.

Chapter Twelve

She cuts through the water like a sheet of gold, touches base at the shallow end, spreads her fingers over the edge and levers herself out. Dripping wet, her watery kiss trickles down my neck onto my dry swimsuit. I shiver.

"Thanks for coming," she says. "I did not know if you would."

"I must be mad," I say, dipping my big toe into the water. "It's freezing in there!"

"Once you're in, it's FANTASTIC! I *promise* you, Sadie," and she dives back in, skims the length of the pool and looks round for me. For a moment, I can't take my eyes off her, bobbing and glistening up the deep end where I hardly ever go, like a beautiful mermaid far out at sea. Cautiously, I climb down the steps into the water and start to swim breaststroke up the pool. People cut across me with butterfly, backstroke, front crawl, churning up the water, churning up my fear. A huge wave hits me in the face, making me splutter and choke. Chlorine stings my throat. Gasping, I stop, feel for the bottom with my feet and, failing to find it, try to get to the side. In my struggle, I catch a glimpse of Anneliese's face at the far end of the pool, solemn and worried, like she's preparing to plunge out and rescue me. I launch out again and this time make it to the steps at the deep end, just as Anneliese's fingers wind around my fingers and draw me in.

Just like that time in the National Gallery when I struggled to get through the crowd to Nu de Dos. The beautiful lady kept drawing me on, willing me to find a way through, and when I reached her, it was incredible.

"Made it," I gasp.

"You made it!" Anneliese says, beaming.

84

She kicks out her legs, tips her head back against the side of the pool and stares up at the roof, dreamily. Strands of her long, auburn hair drift on the water's surface, like stray twigs.

"Watch this," she says, and she pushes away from the side and presses so deeply into the water, I can't see her at all. I push on my goggles and through the watery film spot her spread across the bottom of the pool like a giant starfish, still and silent against the seabed, before she's up, flipping around me, spraying me with water.

At the end of the session, she loops her arms through mine and draws me through the water so smoothly I am like a thread of cotton unravelling from its spool. I close my eyes, letting the water wash over me.

In the cubicle, I sit wrapped in my towel, thinking about our time together in the water. Normally, I'd be scraping myself dry, forcing my clothes over my damp body, desperate to get home. But tonight, I want to linger. Anneliese is getting changed next door. I can hear the rub of towel against her skin, the squeak of her wet Lycra swimsuit being pulled from her body, the crackle of her rucksack, the ping of her twenty pence piece hitting the floor, and then no sounds at all. I wonder if she's lingering too, thinking the same thoughts as me.

"Are you ready, Sadie?" she suddenly calls in her beautifully precise German accent.

"Two minutes," I call back, and have one almighty race to get dressed.

When I come out of my cubicle and lock eyes with her, something's different. It's been different for a while, only I haven't really noticed until this moment. She's not my boyfriend's German Facebook mate any more – the one *I* have to look after cos *he* doesn't want to. She's my own special friend, who understands me in a way other girls don't.

Like, when to mention my dad and when not to, when I feel like talking and when I don't, or when to make me laugh and when to be serious. She knows these things about me, and she accepts and respects them.

Like the other day, after visiting Dad, she knew I needed to talk even before I opened my mouth, and it all came flooding out about how unhappy I am about my parents' divorce, and how I think Bruno's a nerd and don't want him as my stepdad, and how I'm mad with Mum for letting it happen, and furious with Dad for going, and angry with the whole world for expecting me to get over it and move on. Anneliese just touched my arm and said:

"Everyone will tell you how you should feel, Sadie. That is what happened when my folks split for a bit; even our postman told me to keep smiling. But I say you only get over it when *you* are ready to, in *your* time, not *theirs*, and one day, when you least expect it, the sun will come out and you will be happy again. But it takes time, and no-one and nothing can push you there."

I cried then. This seemed the wisest and most special thing anyone had ever said to me.

After the pool, we go our separate ways. Anneliese goes back to Shaun's place, and I go back to Bruno, pumping iron in our hallway. I nearly fall over all his gym equipment but save myself just in time, and instead of scowling manage to conjure a really nice smile.

"You look happy," he says. "Been somewhere nice?"

"Swimming," I say.

"A bit chilly for that, isn't it? It's minus two out there!" and he feigns this huge shiver, as he thrusts his weights into the air.

"It was at first, but once I was in the water, I forgot all about the cold. I'm going again next week."

He gives me an "I'll believe it when I see it" glance and thrusts the weights even higher, this time right above his head. His biceps are unreal!

"In case you're wondering, your mum and Arry are at the supermarket," he hisses, through clenched teeth.

"I guessed so," I say and am about to disappear upstairs when something forces me back. I'm not sure what it is exactly, but it's like one of Bruno's weights clamping down in front of me, and it's not so much a bad feeling as a very, very strong one.

I turn and look at Bruno, whose face is as purple as an aubergine from the strain of the weights and who has his eyes fixed on the ceiling, and I kind of get the feeling he'd find it a lot easier if I just went up to my room and stayed there. But I can't move, and the longer I'm stuck here, the more purple his face gets and the more his hands tremble and quiver under the pressure of the weights, and the weirdest, most out of the blue thought pops into my head: *Bruno's scared stiff of me!*

Crazy, isn't it? A grown man of fifty scared of a teenage girl! I mean, if he's going to be scared of anyone, it should be of my dad for being Mum's ex; or of Greg, the window cleaner, for being built like a brick house and having a huge crush on Mum. But it's not Dad or Greg. It's me! And all the times come flooding back when I've arrived home and Bruno's eyes have flickered nervously, or he's backed away from me and started fiddling with something, and I realise he's not scared I'll do something really nasty to him, like bash him over the head with a saucepan; he's scared of the way I roll my eyes when he cracks a bad joke, or ignore him when he's fishing for a compliment, or tut and groan when he plays his heavy metal. He's scared of me not liking him, not accepting him as my stepdad and only putting up with him because I *have* to. He's scared that, deep down, I might actually *hate* him. And that makes me feel shocked, sad, ashamed and embarrassed all in one go.

The atmosphere between us is terrible – the worst it's *ever* been. Being lodged on the stairs like this, unable to move, knowing what I know, and with Bruno knowing that I know what I know, and with neither of us knowing what to say, makes for mega high tension: the kind which brings Bruno's weights crashing to the floor with an ALMIGHTY THUD. Purple, red and totally embarrassed, we just stand there gawping at them.

"Mum… said… you used to be a really good swimmer," I stutter, "and that once… you even swam for the county."

"… that was when I was a bit younger," he splutters back.

"And that you won a county championship medal when you were younger."

He nods shyly, turns even more purple, and I don't know what to say next.

Until this moment, I have never, ever paid Bruno a compliment. I haven't even hinted he looks nice in his purple velvet jacket or is a whizz on the computer or makes curries to die for. I've never really believed Mum's stories about him winning medals because I've never wanted to admit he could be good at something. I've been too mean and hurt and angry to face the fact that there are things Bruno can do better than my dad, and swimming is one of them.

"You should have seen me in the pool today. I was rubbish. My breaststroke was useless, and my front crawl doesn't even exist! I really admire people who can swim properly, keep their heads down and not crash into things."

"Crawl is only about having the right technique and streamlining yourself," he says, wiping the sweat from his brow and suddenly sounding a lot more confident and looking a lot less terrified. "Once you've got the knack, it's dead easy."

"I wish!" I say.

There's another tense silence, during which I really feel like shooting upstairs, but Bruno wants to talk some more.

"Maybe, when we have a free evening, you and I could take a trip to the pool and work on your front crawl a bit, just so you don't bang your head any time soon."

"Anneliese can help me," I say, quickly brushing off his suggestion. "She's a brilliant swimmer! You should see her in the water… she's like a mermaid… she… yes… yes… that would be great. Thanks, thanks, Bruno."

"Tomorrow, then? I'll have you beating Anneliese in no time."

"I don't want to beat her!" I cry. "I just want to keep pace with her, so we can skim the water together."

"Special friend is she, this Anneliese?"

"Yes," I murmur.

"Tomorrow, at seven p.m. then."

And suddenly the sensation of the lead weight has gone, and I don't feel trapped or ashamed or embarrassed, or anything like that any more. I'm flying through air.

Chapter Thirteen

BOMBSHELL NUMBER SIX… SHAUN FORGETS HIS LINES!

Bang in the middle of his first live performance of *A Midsummer Night's Dream*, in front of his mum and dad, my mum and Bruno, Miss Ferris, most of his teachers, all his school mates and half the town. It's his *worst* nightmare, and instant suicide for his brand new, ultra cool, thespian image. Not even strutting around the stage, looking drop-dead gorgeous in black leather trousers and a midnight-blue velvet cloak half slung across his naked, bronzed chest, can alter the fact that when he opens his mouth to speak, nothing comes out.

Then the prompt forgets to prompt him, and it's left to Miss Ferris, frantic and ten rows back, to bellow: *ill met by moonlight, proud Titania*. Poor, poor Shaun. He's devastated! It takes me the whole thirty minutes of the interval to try to piece him together, and it's hard work, I can tell you. He just flops backstage, his head as droopy as an overcooked cabbage, feeling *utterly* sorry for himself.

"I hate myself, Sadie. I've let everyone down. I wish I'd never been given the part of Oberon."

"You got it because you're the best, Shaun. *Never* forget that."

"That's not what they're saying out there. I've screwed up big time."

"Everyone gets first night nerves, even famous actors. It's normal, Shaun. You'll be better in the second half. Just wait and see."

But then Arabella storms backstage and undoes all my good work.

"Thanks *a lot*, Shaun! You *ruined* that scene for me. You've probably wrecked my entire acting career. What the *hell* were you playing at?"

"I don't know, Arry. I just forgot my lines, didn't I! I couldn't help it."

"How could you forget the most quoted lines in Shakespeare," she snorts imperiously, "when you've been boring me with them for the last two months?"

"Fourth most quoted, actually," I pipe up, "after, *Once more unto the breach*, *To be, or not to be* and *Friends, Romans, countrymen…*

"Fourth, fifth, one hundredth. Who cares! You made me look a total idiot. I'll never forgive you, Shaun. Never!"

"I'm sorry, Arry. Honestly, I am." (He's wheedling now. I hate it when he wheedles. It makes him look all weak and pathetic, and Arabella all powerful and dominant.) "I promise I won't let you down again. I *promise* to be word-perfect by Wednesday night."

"You better be. Otherwise, you can get yourself another Titania!" and she flounces out.

Next day is Wednesday, and for two whole hours after school I don't see Shaun – I just hear him. He locks himself in his bedroom, his head buried in the play and refuses to admit me. I have to test him on his lines through the keyhole. Whenever he makes a mistake, I trot off to the bathroom, while he repeats the line fifty times and then calls me back.

"You know, it's not cool to learn your lines like times tables," I shout through the keyhole. "Real actors don't. They practise scenes with their girlfriends as stand-ins, chill, have a coffee, put their feet up, start again. Why don't you open the door, Shaun, and let me step in as Titania to help you along?"

"But I'm not a *real* actor, am I? I'm just trying to hack it for some dumb school play, so when I walk out on the street, I don't look a total loser. Lose yourself in the loo, will you!"

For the next thirty minutes, I swing my legs on Mrs Wilson's toilet and count the dots on her Laura Ashley wallpaper, and basically kill time while I wait for Shaun. By ten to six, he's word perfect, action perfect, cue perfect. By the start of the live performance, he's not just good, he's BRILLIANT, and Arabella has to eat her words.

Thursday, fifteenth October: girls mob Shaun on his way to school. Shaun laps up all the attention, doles out his autograph like he's Orlando Bloom, and promises fans he'll turn up in leather trousers on Friday.

Friday, sixteenth October: Shaun in black leather trousers is a BIG mistake. Girls go *wild*! One tries to take a chunk out of his thigh, and then four of them grab him by the waist, pin him to the wall and slobber all over him. That's when Shaun goes off fame *fast*. He's fussy about who touches him, you see – and that includes girls with unexpected strength grabbing him from all angles.

Saturday, seventeenth October: last night of the play, followed by cast party. Everyone is here, and the atmosphere is magic. Miss Ferris stands by the door, smoking cigars and smiling lots. The play has been a mammoth success, and she's *very* happy about it. I chat to Anneliese and then make up a group of five on the dance floor. Shaun and Arry are talking again. Once Shaun got his act together, Arabella melted and became all angelic.

Eleven-thirty p.m.: I go to the cloakroom to get my coat and Anneliese's coat. See Shaun and Arabella outside the D&T block. Looks like they're saying goodbye to each other. I'm cool about it. After all, this is the last time they'll see each other for ages. They hug, kiss each other on both cheeks, in that posey way actors do, and Shaun walks off. But then he stops, turns and walks back again and gives Arry another kiss, this time on one cheek, and another hug, which goes on ages. I try not to feel upset. It's normal to get close in a play – pros do all the time and then go back to their own lives. It's just part of coming out of a fantasy world and moving back into the real one. And in some ways, it's no different from Anneliese giving me that kiss in the pool.

I put on my coat and decide that I won't mention their long goodbye to anyone.

Monday, nineteenth October: the play is over. Girls have stopped mobbing Shaun and everything's back to normal – except, that is, for Shaun's mood. It's never been so grim. He mopes around really sullenly, moans when we're with Anneliese, moans when we're not, and snaps my head off whenever I mention Arry's speed dating. I don't believe Mum when she says he's just tired after the play, or Bruno when he says his head has been overinflated by fame and he can't get used to it being normal size again. His grumpiness is a complete conundrum, which I *have* to solve.

So, in between school and taking Sammy to the vet for his annual check-up, I draw up a list of reasons a boy like Shaun, who has *everything* going for him, would be totally miserable:

1. Spurs losing or being relegated to a lower division.
2. Someone Shaun loves dying or being about to die.
3. Shaun's mum and dad having a big bust-up.
4. Shaun's girlfriend (i.e. me) falling out of love with Shaun, or Shaun falling out of love with his girlfriend (i.e. me) and not knowing how to tell her.

And a list of counter reasons:

1. Spurs haven't lost or been relegated to a lower division.
2. Nobody has died or is about to die because Shaun would have told me.
3. Shaun's mum and dad haven't had a bust-up because they never talk, and to have a bust-up you probably have to talk, argue, shout and scream.

Which leaves point number 4. *I* haven't fallen out of love with Shaun, but what about Shaun with me? While sixty per cent of me is pretty certain Shaun's still in love with me, there's this niggling forty per cent which won't go away, and having an imagination as long and winding as the Amazon river it doesn't take long for this forty per cent to become fifty, sixty, seventy, eighty and ninety per cent of me, and I can't rest till I know the truth. I decide to embark on a secret mission to follow Shaun, not so I can spy on him doing stuff he doesn't want me to see, but just to be sure he's not seeing another girl. And I take Sammy with me, in case I need an excuse.

Sammy isn't impressed. He thinks we're going for a proper walk, where he can run free and sniff all the spots where other dogs have done a wee. Instead, he gets put on a lead the length of a sausage and made to walk to heel – all the way down to the sports ground, where Shaun is *meant* to be finishing a game of football. I know I shouldn't really be doing this – it's risky and Shaun would ditch me on the spot if he found out. Far better, though, to take a big risk than be paranoid for the rest of my life.

Phew! Shaun's in goal and looking so incredible with his hair ruffled by the wind and his tanned, muscular body flipping all over the place, I nearly pass out. I yank Sammy behind the nearest pillar and peep round it, my eyes glued to the goal posts. The referee blows his whistle, the game ends, the sides disperse and disappear down a long, narrow tunnel to the changing rooms. Not Shaun, though. He stays put. Nothing unusual in that, I think to myself. Maybe he's not sweaty enough for a shower (I mean, he *is* the sweetest smelling boy on earth), or maybe he prefers his mum's power shower to a useless trickle of a thing.

He doesn't do anything especially strange either, which would make me overly suspicious. He just hangs around, a bit bored and restless, leans against the goal post, does a few arm and leg stretches, leans again, stretches again. The trouble is he's still leaning and stretching twenty minutes later when everyone else has showered, changed and gone home. Now that *is* strange because no matter how big a fitness fanatic Shaun is (and believe me he is – that's why he has *such* a beautiful body), there's no way he'd put fitness before supper at seven p.m. at night!

Suddenly, Sammy lets out this hideous whine, making me jump miles. I shoot behind the pillar, clamp my hand over his muzzle and order him to shut up. He turns his soft brown eyes on me in complete disgust: disgust that I've done him out of a real walk, disgust that I'm not being my usual nice self and putting up with every noise that comes out of his mouth and, most of all, disgust that I'm secretly spying on my boyfriend. Sammy knows everything about me, you see. I can't hide a thing from him.

Totally disgusted, he slumps behind the pillar, and I slump next to him, wishing I'd never embarked on my secret mission, could trust Shaun and didn't have to resort to dirty tactics to prove his love. Two minutes later, Sammy's licking my hand, which means he's forgiven me and is ready to get going. But instead of frisking about and tugging on his lead, he keeps licking me, over and over, like he's trying to tell me something major. That's when I know it's time to face facts once and for all and take another long, hard look at the pitch. And that's when I see Shaun and Arabella inside the goalposts, their faces radiant with moonlight, their hands wandering all over each other. And that's when I very, very nearly pass out.

All I can think about is that scene in *A Midsummer Night's Dream* when Oberon and Titania kiss and make up under Miss Ferris's specially made canvas sky, which is dotted with aluminium foil stars and a huge papier-mâché moon, and how they can't get enough of each other. Only, this is no dream, no play. This is real life, and we're not in a fairy wood, but in a cold, wind-torn stadium, where the wind blasts through the railings and the railings rattle like an old man's bones, and Shaun isn't king of the fairies, playing to his fairy queen. He's himself, a real boy, who has fallen in love – deeply in love – with a real girl, and that girl happens to be my twin.

All the stars are out; I can't count them, there are so many. I glance down at Sammy, sad and forlorn beside me, and think what a fool I was ever to believe Shaun wanted me more than Arabella. Arabella, who'd even look good in a bin bag and who thinks just because she can have nearly any boy on the planet, she can have my boyfriend, too. Arabella, who thinks it's fine to have a quick grope with him inside the goalposts and then go home, pretending nothing has happened. No wonder she's aiming for RADA. She's not just any old actress. She's a *great* one!

I feel in my pocket for a treat for Sammy and slip it into his mouth, before pulling out my phone with the pic of Shaun and me boating on the river. In the dark, sloping shadows, I try to make sense of our happy faces, and the way the sun created shining rings of light on the water, and then I try to make sense of Shaun and Arabella over there, entwined like vines, their faces turned up to the stars and to the cold blue light of the moon, and I think there must be two kinds of happiness: the happiness of being with someone you like (i.e. Shaun with me on the river that day), whose company you enjoy and friendship you cherish, and the second kind of happiness, which is being dotty about someone you can't get out of your head, you're madly in love with and who makes you feel you're in heaven. That's the kind of happiness on Shaun's face now: a sort of supreme, serene, unearthly happiness, making him glow all over like the moon.

I can't face going home. Maybe I'll never go home again. Home is meant to be a safe, secure place; not somewhere lies are told and twin bonds broken. Trembling, I pace up and down my five metres of space, not knowing what to do, and turn out of the sports club and into the park, ending up in the exact spot Shaun and I had our first date, where I licked my Mr Whippy, and Arabella plonked her psychic presence between us. Now there's just Sammy and me, and a huge lump of pain inside me that won't go away.

I can't stop thinking about Shaun and Arabella, wondering if they're still entwined like vines, or in some cosy restaurant, having a cosy time, or if he's sneaked her back to his house and they're up in his bedroom, *doing things*.

I try not to think *too* much about them *doing things* because that makes the lump of pain worse, but every time I don't think about it, I think about it more, till I feel like I'm going out of my mind and have to phone Anneliese on my mobile.

"I'm in the park with Sammy. Something's happened… with Shaun," I blubber.

There's a silence the length of the Channel Tunnel.

"Shaun? He is not dead, Sadie?"

"No, he's not dead, but he's done something with Arabella behind my back. They're off somewhere, doing it right now!"

I'm not sure how much sense Anneliese can make of my gabble because phrases like *behind my back*, *off somewhere* and *doing it* could well be difficult for a German girl to understand. But she's even more switched on than I realise.

"Stay calm, Sadie. Stay *very*, *very* calm. I will cycle over to the park immediately. You must wait for me at the seat. Do not leave. Do not talk to strangers. It will be all right. Just wait with Sammy until I arrive."

When Anneliese gets to me, I'm shaking and shivering so much I can't talk. She winds her woollen scarf around my neck and takes hold of Sammy. Then she gives me the best advice ever – to go straight home – which I do because it feels like minus three in the park and there's only one thing worse than a broken heart and that's a bad case of hypothermia, followed by rapid death. As Anneliese walks with me to the house, I start to feel calmer, as though I'm being guided by a steady bright star.

"You will come and see me tomorrow?" I say, weakening under Sammy's tug to get inside.

Nodding, she tells me to be brave and, mounting her bike, vanishes into the night.

Bruno's in the kitchen, stirring a hot Ribena for his cold. I never thought I'd say this, but I'm overjoyed to see him. In his navy towelling bathrobe and old floppy slippers, he makes everything seem normal (even if it isn't). What's more, he acts quite normally, saying how tough his day has been and how he can't wait to hit the sack extra early. When he's gone, I feel anxious. I sit at the kitchen table with my bowl of Shredded Wheat and hot milk, as I always do after a night out. But really I'm waiting, terrified, for Arabella to walk through the door. Will she come and talk to me or slink upstairs guiltily? Will I smile sweetly at her or shove her face into my Shredded Wheat? I don't know what she'll do or what I'll do. How can I know such things when I don't know what's true or false any more? I thought I *knew* my twin, *knew* my boyfriend and *knew* where I stood with each of them. I *trusted* them. It turns out I don't know them and can't trust them at all.

"Sadie… Sadie," a sweet voice is whispering to me in a dream. There's someone's hand on the back of my head, and a warm, soggy feeling on my face and foot. I've fallen asleep over my bowl of Shredded Wheat, and it's tipped over. The milk's dribbling down the table leg onto my foot and someone very kind is trying to stop the flow with one hand and stroke my hair with the other. It's a blissful sensation of being halfway between sleeping and waking, absorbed in a land of milk and honey, where everything is warm and wet and hazy, and the sweet, familiar sounds of everyday life filter through softly, without any of the nasty bits. I want to stay in this world of soft yellow light, where words caress me like musical notes and there's no pain and no unhappiness, because it's here I feel absolutely safe.

"Sadie… Sadie… wake up, darling. You've been fast asleep."

Bleary-eyed, I contemplate this angel who has slipped into my honey world and is gently stroking me. The angel picks up the dishcloth and starts mopping up the milk. Behind her, a second, dimmer angel surfaces, his head bent low, as if he's saying a prayer. I rub the sleep from my eyes to make the vision clearer and see not two angels, but Arabella and Shaun!

"Hi, Sadie," Shaun says, raising his hand to me and dropping it like a guillotine.

"Shaun! What are you doing here?" I exclaim.

"Thought I'd drop by to see you after football practice, didn't I," he says, "and I bumped into Arabella on the doorstep."

Somehow, Shaun saying this triggers the night's events and they come flooding back to me, like a series of fast moving, high colour digital images, crude and garish, and I know for a fact Shaun's lying through his teeth.

"Not true! You didn't drop by to see *me,* and you didn't bump into Arabella on the doorstep, either!"

"What do you mean?" he mumbles, embarrassed.

"What I say! You can't fool me, Shaun. I saw you and Arabella together on the football pitch."

"You *what*?"

"I said I saw you and Arabella on the football pitch, groping each other. It was disgusting. I was there with Sammy, and he saw you, too!"

"God, Sadie, what are you saying?" Arabella mutters, and she glares at Shaun so murderously I'm surprised he doesn't just drop down dead. "What do you mean you *saw* us? When exactly?"

"Tonight, at seven p.m. You two couldn't keep your hands off each other."

"Sure," she proclaims, really cockily. "Like Shaun and I would meet for a quick grope on a freezing cold football pitch in full view of the world. Get real, Sadie!"

And she does that thing I hate (which she always does when she's losing an argument) of sticking her boobs out so hard, they become mini torpedoes, aimed straight at me.

"What's that, then?" I say, pointing to the nasty, purply-red splodge rising between her torpedoes, a dead giveaway if ever I saw one. It sits on her skin like a squashed strawberry, little pinpricks of blood framing its edges like strawberry seeds. Shaun always said he couldn't stand love bites – that they were cheap and nasty, and he'd never lower himself to give one. Well, unless my eyes deceive me, he's had a *major* change of heart because this one's worthy of Count Dracula!

"Don't tell me you fell over and hit your boob on a stone because I just won't believe you!" I say.

Arabella gives a little start and dips her head to the nasty red splodge, bulging and throbbing beneath her skin and then (unbelievably) yanks up her jumper to try to hide it. Only, it's too late for cover-ups. All her guilt is seeping from her, like thick, mushy strawberry juice, making me feel utterly sick.

"Oh, Sadie, I'm *so* sorry. I *never* meant to hurt you. It was the play that did it. I tried to warn Shaun off, but the play kept pushing us closer and closer together, and every time I backed away Miss Ferris said we weren't acting like *real* lovers and could we try the love scene again and *really* hot it up. I tried, I *really* did try not to feel anything, but every time Shaun kissed me all these feelings welled up from deep inside – feelings I didn't even know were there – and I couldn't stop them!"

"Like hell! It's not Miss Ferris's fault. It's yours! You couldn't stand me going out with Shaun and you used the play to get him back. You couldn't stand me having a boyfriend when you didn't have one!"

"No, no!" she cries. "I didn't know I wanted Shaun. I thought I was in love with Alex, but then Alex did what he did, and during rehearsals Shaun was so kind and supportive, I realised Alex was just a stupid crush I was over, and Shaun was for real. I *never* meant to hurt you, Sadie. I *tried* and *tried* to tell you but didn't know how!"

"Oh, yeah, and I suppose you're madly in love with each other and in two years' time you're going to get married, have loads of babies and live happily ever after."

She fixes her sky-blue eyes on me with the kind of certainty that makes my blood run cold. Four years from now I could be babysitting their kids while they go out for smoochy candlelit dinners. I could be staying overnight in their house, listening to them having sex next door!

Suddenly, it feels like a thick cord is wound around my neck, getting tighter and tighter, and I can hardly breathe.

"Say something, Sadie. I don't like it when you go all quiet," Arabella cries.

I stare at Shaun and Arabella. Shaun's pupils are monstrous black dials, dilating and submerging the watery green of his irises. Soon there will be nothing left of Shaun of the oceanic eyes.

"What's there to say?"

"Anything!" Arabella pleads. "Just don't stay mute because that really scares me."

But it seems that everything that needs to be said, has been said. Shaun and Arabella are in love and one day they'll get married and have kids. Those are the facts, and nothing I say now will change any of that. Somehow, there doesn't seem any point in sitting at the kitchen table with my twin whimpering and running her hands through her for once greasy hair, and my ex-boyfriend gawping at me like I'm an apparition. There's no point at all, so I get up and make for the door.

"*Say something, Sadie!*" Arabella screeches.

I freeze in the doorway.

"OK, I'll say something. BITCH!" I say and walk out.

Chapter Fourteen

I wander through the streets, not knowing where I'm heading. At midnight I think about Mum, frantic with worry, and decide to go back. She doesn't say a word, but from the look on her face I can tell she knows everything. She steers me up to her bedroom, sits me on her bed and wraps a soft, warm fleece around my shoulders. Her love comes through to me in heavy sighs and tight, bandage-like hugs and firm, definite strokes of my face. Sammy appears in the doorway, hops onto the bed and starts licking me. I lean against him. He is soft and strong, like a mossy tree trunk which stops me falling. I rest my hand on his back and pray he'll never get sick and die. Even now I can't cry; I should be able to, but the tears won't come. Instead, I retch onto the fleece. "It's the cold and the shock," Mum says. "It was a harsh thing to do to you and I've said so." That's when the tightness in my throat and chest starts to ease slightly and I feel I can breathe again.

Mum runs me a salt bath, helps me to undress and steadies me while I climb in. The water is a deep-blue lagoon, soothing away my pain. Fleetingly, I think of Anneliese, the mermaid in the pool, drawing me through the water effortlessly.

"You can sleep in my bed tonight," Mum says. "Sammy can stay with you, if you like."

"What about Bruno? What about the house rules?" I ask.

"Bruno's agreed to take the spare room… and the house rules, well… they hardly apply any more. I just… I just want you to feel safe and happy in your own home, Sadie," and she sobs into my bath water.

I sleep curled up with Sammy. He pants a lot and won't settle, but my sleep is broken anyway by terrible flashbacks to the football ground, and thoughts of Arabella, alone and guilt-ridden next door. The following morning Mum tells me what's happening.

"Arabella's going to stay at Great Aunt Eva's for a few days. It's all been arranged and she's fine about it. It will give you both the space you need."

Great Aunt Eva's, I think; that hideous Gothic mansion in the depths of the Berkshire countryside, where the sun never shines, and ghosts lurk around every corner, and the television never, ever goes on.

"Oh," I say.

"I know it's hard to take this on board, Sadie, and I'm not trying to excuse Arabella, but she's very upset and feels very ashamed about what she's done."

"I know," I say.

But that doesn't mean I can just forgive her. She and Shaun have broken my heart, and it'll take more than a few days to mend, if ever.

For the next two days it rains solidly, as if some spiteful weather goddess up in the sky knows it's the start of half-term and wants to ruin it for teenagers everywhere. In a funny kind of way though, I find it comforting to be tucked up indoors with the fire roaring, and the rain savagely lashing the windowpanes.

I dip into all my favourite poets: Wordsworth, Christina Rossetti, Wendy Cope.

I think of Shaun.

I flick through Mum's magazines.

I think of Shaun.

I stuff myself with melted marshmallows.

I think of Shaun.

I talk to Mum about what's happened.

I think of Shaun.

I think of Arabella playing scrabble with Great Aunt Eva and pity her.

I think of Shaun.

I think of Shaun and Arabella together and stop pitying Arabella.

I talk to Bruno about swimming.

I think of Shaun.

I phone Dad and cry down the phone.

I phone Anneliese and cry down the phone.

I think of Shaun and nearly pick up the phone.

I think of Shaun of the mellifluous voice and oceanic eyes and wish things had never changed between us; wish we were still up in that dusty, musty attic, making music on our instruments, and in our souls. Then I remember it will never be like that again, and I force myself to stop thinking about him.

A text comes through from Shaun on Tuesday, full of stuff I'd rather not read.

> Sadie, please forgive me. I never meant to cheat on you. Nor did Arry. I really respect you. You're kind and clever and loyal and mega talented. I meant it when I said I like you exactly as you are. But Arry and me, well, we're right for each other, I guess. I hope you meet someone really special because you deserve to. I hope we can still be friends. Love Shaun.

I delete it top speed.

**

Arabella takes an age to come back from Great Aunt Eva's, and no-one, except me, knows why – she's too scared to come home and face me. Mum says a week is the maximum amount of time any boy should split up twins, even if a huge cesspit of hurt and anger is swishing between them. But I'm in no mood to make up. Everywhere I look – in the park, in the cinema, in the house, in my head – all I see are Shaun and Arabella groping. My head's turned into grope city. I can't even take a trip to Ikea without thinking of Shaun and Arry in a big Swedish bed, making babies.

But I do go to the swimming pool. There's not too much to upset me here because groping couples are banned, and Shaun can't swim anyway. Once I slip into the water, an extraordinary change comes over me. Pockets of water slap and lap against all the jammed-up unhappiness in my heart and set it flowing into the mighty ocean of the pool. I forget all my hurt and just glide on the surface weightlessly, like a float.

Anneliese glides beside me, her face tipped towards mine. She's amazed by the improvement in my swimming. Less than four weeks ago, I was just splashing and crashing about in the shallow end. Now, she says, I'm ready for Munich's Olympic pool, and texts her German friends to say so.

I say, "Hang on, I'm hardly a pro, you know; just an amateur, who's proved she can swim a lot better than she thought!" But she won't let up. She's giddy with my progress, and ecstatic that Bruno made me come down here on dark autumn nights to practise. The more she praises me, the more excited I get, till I'm high on thoughts of lazy, summer days by sun-drenched German lidos, and coffee and kuchen at the water's edge, and meandering through Munich's Italianate buildings at twilight, with Anneliese by my side.

"You really want me to come to Germany?" I say.

"Sure," she replies, slipping away into her watery depths.

Long before any trip to Germany though, I invite Anneliese over to my house. Now Shaun's out of the picture, it makes sense for us to spend more time together. She comes with two cans of ginger beer, a giant packet of tortilla chips and her iPod with a load of music downloads, all stuffed into her rucksack. In some ways, it's like having any friend over. We guzzle the ginger beer and tortilla chips, listen to the music, watch an episode of *Friends,* and then she asks to see my bedroom.

Now, not many people have been in my bedroom. It's my private space only a few people enter: like Mum, and Sammy (before the ban), and Arry when we were speaking. And even though I went into Shaun's bedroom loads of times and lay down on his bed while he fondled different bits of me, he hasn't so much as put his big toe over the threshold of *my* room. Come to think of it, I don't think he's even been upstairs.

So, when Anneliese asks point blank to see my bedroom, it's a shock and I nearly choke on my ginger beer. But that's Anneliese for you – blunt in a way most girls aren't. While at times this can be very embarrassing, it's also useful because it means I can be blunt back without worrying about what happens; which means I could give a straight "NO!" to this bedroom question and we could stay downstairs all afternoon, lounging around and watching comedies. But, in fact, what I give is a straight "YES!".

We climb the stairs and enter. Fortunately, Anneliese likes my room, and her approval makes a warm, frothy feeling bubble up inside me. Blue happens to be her favourite colour, and she likes the way my turquoise mesh curtains shimmer in the heat of the radiator, and my miniature perfume bottles form a half-moon around my dressing table, and my family photos take up nearly an entire wall – though she doesn't say too much about these; just glances at them and passes on. What *I* like is the way she's interested in all my stuff but doesn't prod and poke and fiddle with it. Then she spots *Nu de Dos* hanging in the shadow of the wardrobe, and she leans towards her, spellbound, as though she's moving further and further into her mystery, and I have a real struggle to get her back.

"Anneliese… Anneliese… are you all right?" I keep calling.

"Fine," she murmurs softly, turning towards me. In her eyes is that same look of light she had in the café – the one which compels me to look away.

"Your print is *beautiful*, Sadie. Zo very, *very* beautiful."

Excitement ripples down my spine.

"I bought it in the National Gallery," I say. "It's from an exhibition that's still on there. I could easily get you one and post it to Germany, if you like."

"Would you, for me?"

"Sure," I whisper.

She studies the picture for a few more seconds and then, with all the grace and poise it possesses, slowly turns on her heel and eases herself onto the edge of my bed. Silently, I ease myself beside her. Some extraordinary atmosphere has taken hold in my room, consisting of Anneliese and *Nu de Dos* and me: so rarefied and highly charged, I sense the slightest sound or movement could break it.

The next thing I know, Anneliese is crying. No, not crying. Sobbing. Tears are drenching her face, her neck, her shirt, the tops of her jeans, and my heart is thumping. I try to comfort her by stroking her arm, but her tears fall in torrents, and so I wrap my arms around her and hold her till they stop. I feel the wet sponginess of her hair sticking to my face, the thick, heavy trickle of her tears running down my neck, the hot point of her cheek bone pressed into mine, the feathery wisps of her breath, warm on my face as she mumbles "… zo zorry, Sadie," and the huge heave of her body as she lets go against me.

Gently, I wipe away her tears, daring to look into her eyes, and that same look is there – watery, shining, intensely beautiful – and this time I don't look away. And it's a look of love and makes me want to draw Anneliese close and kiss her, and suddenly I *am* kissing her: her cheeks, her eyes, her neck, her lips, properly, completely, like I've never kissed anyone before. Like I've never *wanted* to kiss anyone before. What's more, *she's* kissing me back.

There's no grinding noise like with Shaun, and no picture in my head of a bus trundling round and round the same old boring route, and no chance either of someone walking in and disturbing us. Her kisses are different from all of that. *They're out of this world.*

But then she pulls away, gives me a confused, bewildered look, mumbles something about Shaun and being late and, before I know it, she's speeding off on her bike, her red, chunky hair bouncing and billowing behind her. Dazed, I watch her go, wondering if I'll ever see her again. For a whole hour I lie on my bed, breathing in the space where she sat, thinking about no-one and nothing else, faint with the sensation of her kisses and the lemony scent of her skin on my skin. When Mum and Bruno get back from Ikea at four p.m., I snap shut the lid on my thoughts and go downstairs.

Mum instantly comments how flushed I look and insists on taking my temperature. As she presses the thermometer under my tongue, I try to behave like nothing has happened, but in the wall mirror huge red blotches are creeping across my face. I'd be worried, think I'd contracted some nasty, skin-creeping disease which is taking over my whole body, if I didn't know otherwise and couldn't see that my general demeanour, far from being disease-ridden, is a glistening orb of light.

"That's funny," Mum says, holding up the thermometer. "I could have sworn you had a temperature. What were you *doing* upstairs?"

"Nothing!" I blurt, so loudly Bruno stops rooting in his Ikea bags and glances up. I can't look at him.

"It's a bit hot in here. I'm going into the garden," I say.

I force on my wellingtons and stagger down to the large, overgrown area Mum calls her wild patch and Bruno calls the *mess*, and start digging like mad: weeds, flowers, soil, stones, anything that will come up. It's the craziest thing to do because Mum knows only too well I can't tell a weed from a wallflower, and it would take something really drastic to make me pick up a spade in the first place. But I had to get out of the house, away from all the questions brewing like beer in there, and into the fresh air. I'm confused enough without having questions fired at me right, left and centre.

I didn't know I was going to kiss Anneliese – I just invited her round. I didn't know anything like *that* was going to happen. It just did, like a gigantic wave which stole up, tossed itself right under me, flung me sky-high and dropped me, floundering, in mid-ocean. Two weeks ago, everything was safely shored: Shaun was my regular boyfriend, Arabella and I were speaking, and Anneliese was just a friend. My life was clear-cut, steady and straightforward. I was happy in an ordinary, safe kind of way. Now I'm not happy at all. I'm more than happy and less than it; high one minute, terrified and rock-bottom the next. I can't stop thinking about Anneliese, but when I do I feel guilty and ashamed.

Digging is no help because no matter how much I hack and shovel and furrow and press, these actions don't stop the feelings growing inside me, and now the wave is stealing towards me again, vast, inflated, coming at me from nowhere, so thick and fast I have to clutch the spade extra hard in case I'm knocked over and Mum and Bruno come charging out, demanding to know the truth. Anneliese's mermaid face swims before my eyes. I long to reach out and touch it; run my fingers over her lips and do the kind of thing I've *never, ever* done with any boy.

"Door, Sadie!" Mum bellows from the house.

I freeze, my body locked between the spade handle and the earth. *The door*! *Someone's at the door*! What if it's Anneliese, back to tell me just now was a big mistake and she never wants to see me again? Or, scarier still, that just now was the best thing *ever* and can we do it again soon?

"Door, Sadie!" Mum bellows. I plunge the spade into the ground, shout "I'm coming," and with my wellies clicking and clacking against my sweaty calves, trudge round to the side gate.

And for what? For creepy, putty-smelling Faz (minus one ferret), whom I thought I'd seen the back of weeks ago! I don't know whether to laugh or cry. His whole body quivers when he sees me – maybe it's because of my red cheeks or pink wellington boots or the clash of red and pink, or the hostile glower on my face – and he goes into mumble mode and starts picking at his fingernails. Mum ushers us into the sitting room, closes the door firmly and leaves us to get on with it. Whatever *it* is.

"Great house," Faz says, eyeing our sitting room with his usual wildness. "Been here long?"

"Sixteen years – the length of my life, Faz."

As his gaze trips from Mum's gold candlesticks to Bruno's crystal pyramid perched on top of the mantelpiece, my imagination trips too, and I wonder if as well as being a putty-smelling, lager-drinking ferret keeper, Faz might also be a thief. Maybe he's using me as a pretext to get into our house and size it up, before making a raid at midnight when everyone's asleep. But this thought doesn't last long, because suddenly his eyes are on me and me *only*.

"Probably wondering why I'm here, aren't you, Sadie?"

"I am really, Faz," I reply, dreading the answer.

"Probably wondering how I know your address and why I'd turn up on your doorstep, chat up your mum and then ask to see you. Probably wondering what would draw me from the midst of my urban life in Guildford to a little town in the countryside, twelve miles away."

"I am really, Faz."

"Well, your wondering is over, Sadie. I'm here because I couldn't stay away a second longer. I've finally plucked up the courage to tell you to your face that I fancy you like mad, fancied you the first time I ever set eyes on you, and will you go out with me?"

What do I say?

"*I'm sorry but you're not my type, Faz.*"

or

"*Sorry, Faz, but I already have a boyfriend.*"

or

"*Sorry, Faz, but I'm allergic to putty, bad breath, lager and ferrets,*" (but he might just promise to take more showers, use a mouth wash, chuck the lager and send Turpin, the ferret, to an animal home).

Or do I tell him the truth that, actually, I'm in love with a girl?

"I can't, Faz," I say.

"Oh, no? Why's that, then?" he mutters, inching closer and closer to me.

"I just can't. Don't ask me the reason. I'm sorry, Faz."

"Bet that's not what you said to Shaun Wilson. Bet you were right up against him faster than I can say *Got yer!*"

And suddenly Faz has *got* me, and I'm right up against him, only an inch from his red, slimy lips, and his breath is coming at me, hot and foul as rotting faggots.

"There's no such word as *'can't'*, Sadie. Don't they teach kids *anything* in school these days?"

I nearly scream, but don't. But not screaming means Faz pulls me even closer, so that his whole body wriggles and writhes against mine like a headless snake. It's disgusting! I can't stand it, and suddenly the truth is tripping off my tongue faster than a meteor hurtling through space.

"I can't go out with you, Faz, because I'm gay."

His mouth drops right open and gets stuck in this oval shape, just like a fish, and between his yellow teeth his slimy, purple tongue wriggles in disbelief.

"Never!" he gasps, loosening his grip on me and dodging sideways.

"Yes." I nod furiously.

"*You?*"

"Yes."

"Since when?"

"Since… since… this afternoon."

"Why? When? Where? How? *Who with?*"

"I can't say, Faz."

"What, a quaint little thing like you?"

"Yes."

"Sure you can't tell me?"

"Positive, Faz."

"Not even the tinciest, winciest hint for poor old Faz, to lift him out of his misery?"

Then something bold and reckless flips open in me.

"Well, if you must know, her name is Anneliese, she's sixteen, comes from Germany, was with me the night of the Jolly

Frog, I fancy her like crazy and we've already snogged. So, there you go, Faz."

A crafty look engulfs Faz's face.

"Does your mum know?"

"Nope."

"Your twin?"

"Nope."

"Your dad?"

"Nope."

"Anyone?"

"Nope. Just you, Faz."

His crafty look erupts into this really smug beam, and I know that by midnight tonight every pub in every town within a twenty-mile radius of Guildford will know my secret, which I've only known for two hours myself!

"Guess that rules me out as your boyfriend, then. But I'm honoured, Sadie. *Really* honoured to be told first. Won't breathe a word – promise," and he gives a huge tap to the side of his nose, as though it's the best secret he's ever been given. Then he ambles across the sitting room, out through the front door, down the drive and he's gone, out of my house, out of my life, taking my secret with him.

Whenever I think I've made a humongous mistake telling Faz my secret, all I have to do is imagine his tongue wriggling around my mouth, and green bits of pea and cabbage escaping from his teeth and getting stuck in my gums, and I know I've done *exactly* the right thing. Telling Faz the truth was the *only* way to get rid of him!

No offence, Faz.

Chapter Fifteen

Arabella finally gets back from Great Aunt Eva's a week late, as flat as a pancake and without saying a word. All she does is stay cooped up in her room, her head stuck in Great Aunt Eva's battered old books, and only comes out when she has to, i.e. when Mum calls her down for a meal or she needs to use the loo, and then she takes all the battered old books with her.

Mum does her best to reinstate the *real* Arabella by tempting her with caramel Magnums and flashing glossy holiday ads in front of her eyes, but Arabella's having none of it. She'd rather shut herself off. No-one knows what's going on in her head, because when she speaks, instead of common sense coming out all you get is this ranting on life, the universe and everything in it. Her trip to Great Aunt Eva's isn't so much shrouded in mystery as marinated in it. Nobody can get to the bottom of *it* or *her*, and Mum's finding it tough.

"We don't want you to be like this!" Mum exclaims. "We want you to be *yourself*, your old self, the Arry we know and love."

"Too right!" Bruno pipes up, who's just about had enough of Arry's ways and is edging closer and closer to the front door.

When Shaun rings her mobile, all hell's let loose. She stares at his name flashing and dancing on the screen, like it's a little red demon about to leap out and bop her on the nose. Then she chucks down the phone and runs out, leaving me to pick up the pieces – Shaun's pieces, that is, not the mobile's.

I must be a complete wally. Six months on, a boyfriend down the drain and a sultry German goddess of a girlfriend shimmering on the horizon, and I'm still a pawn in Arabella's little dramas. Shaun, of course, is overjoyed to get me on the line – better to get the twin he dumped than the angry mum or even angrier stepdad. At least with me he's got a slim chance of wangling his way back into Arry's life, whereas with Bruno he's got zero chance. But what sort of boy would use the twin he's dumped to get back with the twin he fancies? Only a sick or desperate one, and *boy* is Shaun desperate! I can hear it in his voice when he tries to butter me up and sweet-talk me into winning Arry round. For a moment I nearly succumb to his dulcet tones, before his voice changes, sharply and forever, and I see sense.

"She won't take my calls, Sadie. It's driving me mad!" he says.

"So?" I say, my heart as hard as an acorn.

"I don't know what to do!"

"She thinks you're a red, fiery demon about to prod her with your pitchfork. She thinks if she goes anywhere near you, she'll roast to death in red-hot flames. She thinks you're the DEVIL, Shaun!"

"Why?" Shaun moans. "I've done nothing to hurt her. The only person I've been devilish to is you!"

There's this horrible silence then, because no way am I expecting Shaun to refer to *us,* and it knocks me off my perch.

"I can't help you, Shaun. Arabella doesn't want to see you and that's that," and I cut him off in mid-groan.

There's not another bleep from him for a whole hour, but by ten forty-five he's bombarding Arry's mobile with droopy, drooly messages of unrequited love.

Life's dross without you, Arry.

Shaun without Arry is like oats without honey.

Make my life, Arry. Come back to me.

All of which go unnoticed by Arabella, who's just about vacated her relationship with everyone and everything: Shaun, her mobile, her family, the whole world. Don't know where she is, but it's certainly not at fifty-six, Heathcote Drive.

Still, if her head's not here with us, her moods are still casting their gloom. Mum and Bruno are having humongous rows. I feel sick all the time. Sammy spends his days cowering under the kitchen table. Nighttime isn't much better. Domestic discord has quadrupled Bruno's snores; if they get much louder, the whole house will cave in. I don't know how Mum stands it with her extra sensitive ear pressed up against his right nostril, which is how it is the night I sneak into their room to retrieve my slippers. For a second, I feel all protective of Mum, and have to give myself a quick jab in the arm to remind myself that she's a grown woman of forty-nine, who actually *fancies* Bruno and *wants* him in her bed.

Heading back to my own room, I meet Arabella on the landing, kitted out in a pair of Dad's old, striped pyjamas. The last time we came face to face in the middle of the night was during the phantom pregnancy scare. If she's going to tell me she's pregnant with Shaun's baby and can I be live-in babysitter, she can forget it! But no, she hasn't even seen me. She's streaking past me, down the stairs into the kitchen. I follow her, taking each stair with the stealth and cunning of a Siamese cat, and stop just short of the kitchen to watch what she does. She opens the cupboard, takes out the packet of Shredded Wheat and a blue china bowl, takes the milk from the fridge and a spoon from the drawer, and lines them all up in a neat row on the kitchen table. Then she sits down in the exact chair I occupied that fatal night I saw them together, but instead of eating the cereal she just loops her hands around the empty bowl and stares at Mum's yellow curtains for a good five minutes. Then she puts everything away and goes back upstairs to bed.

"Sleepwalking," Dad says, when I tell him about it on the phone next day. "Kathy's Becky did it when her kid brother fell out of a moving train. Kid brother was OK – not a bone out of place – but poor Becky wasn't. She went rambling around that old London house in the early hours of the morning for well over a year. I should tell Mum, if I were you."

Two days later, there's something else: Dr Roberts's green check jacket pressed up against the glass door of our conservatory, and

Mum pacing up and down, up and down. I don't like the look of this, so I slip into the kitchen to escape. Next thing I know, Mum's standing right behind me.

"Sadie, Dr Roberts is here to see Arabella. She's not well and there's something I want you to do."

Something I want you to do. Mum's words grip me like a convulsion. I try to keep things light by casually offering her one of my marmalade squares, but really my stomach is knotting and I'm breaking out in this terrible sweat. *Something I want you to do.*

"What?" I ask, nonchalantly.

"Talk to Arabella and tell her you still love her and forgive her for what she did to you, because that's her only chance of coming out of this nightmare and being well again."

I don't even know what's wrong with Arabella. All I know is she's sleepwalking and acting like never before. I can't actually say to friends she has X, Y or Z, or look her 'illness' up in a medical dictionary, because so far it hasn't been given a name by Mum or Doctor Roberts or anyone. Nobody's made any attempt to explain it to me, and yet, in the midst of this baffling mystery, which is giving Mum a permanent headache, tipping Bruno in the direction of the front door and plunging Sammy into dog depression, *I'm* the person called upon to make Arabella better, when maybe not even God himself could do it!

"Why can't Dr Roberts just give her some pills?" I ask.

Mum shakes her head solemnly.

"It's not that simple, Sadie. She needs to know *you* love her and forgive her. She *really* needs to believe that. She feels so guilty about what she did to you, it's making her ill. You're the only person who can take away that guilt. A pill can't."

"But I didn't ask her to be ill! *I'm* the one who's suffering. She did that terrible thing to me, not me to her! Why should *I* be the one to make her better?"

Mum's hands are covering her face, so I can't see the expression

116

in her eyes or make out what she's thinking, and everything is getting darker and scarier by the second.

"Please, Sadie," she pleads, uncovering her eyes and staring at me through a grey, deathly cloud of despair. "I know it's hard, but this is *very* serious, so *please* just talk to her," and she shuffles from the kitchen like an old woman of one-hundred-and-five, and I'm left with Sammy, who doesn't even raise his head off the floor to comfort me.

The front door slams. Dr Roberts goes off in his car. Bruno revs his engine hard and follows. No-one comes near the kitchen. I feel like a criminal who's committed such an appalling crime, everyone's avoiding me. I feel guilty and angry and alone, and I shouldn't have any of these feelings because none of this is my fault! Once again, Arabella has let me down BIG TIME. Once again, she's twisted the truth into such an ugly, warped knot, it looks like *I'm* the one to blame, while *she's* poor little Miss Innocent. Tell her now that I love her and it'll be my biggest act yet. I'll be doing it for Mum, not because I mean it. Mum didn't say tell Arabella you love her and really *mean* it. She just said tell her you love her. So maybe that's what I'll do: just go through the motions, speak the words.

Footsteps heave and creak above me. Mum's going for a lie-down. When she wakes, she'll expect me to have done the *thing*. I cram the last two marmalade squares into my mouth and remain lodged to the kitchen units, stubbornly chewing. Outside, in the garden, bare tree branches are gathering like rubble, and puddles are turning to hard, icy wedges. Inside, in the sitting room opposite, Arabella is curled up on the sofa, a small, black bundle of a thing.

OK, so she's not her usual self, and that tiny stomach bulge now goes in rather than out, and there are thick, black bags under her eyes. But that's hardly serious. Serious is Callie Mitton smashing up a whole kitchen after her dad was sent to prison and then trying to kill herself. Or Callie Mitton kicking down the neighbour's fence and screaming the F word so many times, the police and social worker are called. It is not black bags and thinness; not midnight jaunts to the kitchen. Lots of girls are thin and lots of girls sleepwalk. Arabella's no different, and all this is one of her classic stunts to get the sympathy off me and onto her, so she can reign supreme again. Well, I'm sick of it!

Sammy sniffs the air hungrily. He's hungry all the time these days: wolfs a huge dinner of meaty chunks and then goes scavenging in recycled food bags for any scraps he can find, leaving a long, messy trail up the driveway. Bruno's not happy till he's brushed, hosed and polished the tarmacadam. Mum's not happy then. She says she wishes Arabella would scavenge for food, instead of shoving it up her sleeve and getting rid of it when she thinks no-one's looking.

Now Sammy is whining by the kitchen door. I know exactly what he wants – he wants to see Arabella.

"*She* doesn't want you," I say, pushing the door wide and watching him bound into the sitting room, where he nearly knocks Arabella off the sofa. I'm right, too. She doesn't want him. She plain ignores him; acts like he doesn't even exist. Won't even stretch out her hand to pat his head. All she does is lie there, cold and silent as a tombstone.

"Oi!" I shout from the doorway. "Your dog is *trying* to get your attention, in case you hadn't noticed!"

Sammy goes berserk. He can't stand being ignored, especially by someone he loves. For him, it's as bad as being pestered when he wants to get to sleep. Like a great she-lion with one of her cubs, he nudges and nuzzles Arabella, rubs against her, licks her bare legs all over. Then his great paws are up on the sofa; his thick, pointed claws are digging into it, and his great, golden head swinging manically between the two of us. His moist brown eyes are landing on me, huge and heavy, like a series of punches, and all the time Arabella is disappearing deeper and deeper into the sofa.

"Don't Sammy. She doesn't want you, boy," I cry, trying to call him off.

Strangely, he obeys me, slumps to the floor and rests his muzzle on Arabella's bare feet. He's never looked so sad, and Arabella's never… I'm walking into the sitting room now, right up to her, forcing myself to look at her not with sideways glances or from under the veil of my fringe, but full on. I'm studying her hard, absorbing every inch of her, trying to work out what all the fuss is about… and I see… *I see she's never looked so ill.*

She's scrunched up on the sofa, like a crushed paper doll. Her eyes, deep ghostly hollows, bore through me without seeing me. Her arms hang from her shoulders like pipe cleaners. Her hands are as pale and fragile as ice cream wafers. Any second now, bits of her might start to flake off, like paper strips from a papier-mâché model. All the time I've been pretending nothing is seriously wrong with her, she's been getting more and more ill. All the time I've been wallowing in my own hurt and sadness, her sadness has been eating away at her. Suddenly, I can see none of this is put on. It's for real, it's getting worse, and if I don't act fast, I won't just have a shadow for a twin, I'll have no twin at all.

In my head I'm saying over and over: *I love you, Arry. I forgive you.* I'm doing what Mum has asked me to do and really meaning it – in my head. But the words won't come: they stay trapped beneath my tongue, and even if they did come, what if Arry's beyond reach? What if she's slipped away into some dark, closed-off place within her own head, where no-one can reach her and from which there's no return? Once, we were close. So close, we could read each other's thoughts. Now it's like trying to read the thoughts of a stranger. There's a thick wall between us, and no matter how much I try to force my thought waves through, they just rebound on me.

Desperate, I kneel beside her and grope for her tiny hand. Catching it, it crumples in mine, like a newborn baby's. I'm summoning all my strength, trying to push the warmth from my veins into hers; trying to force the message through that I'm here and

I LOVE HER. I'll stay like this for hours if I have to, just to get a sign, any sign, she's still with me.

It feels like I wait forever. Mum finishes her nap and starts moving around her bedroom. Bruno comes into the house and goes out again. Sammy sinks into a deep, deep sleep. I feel like screaming and shouting, the pain of waiting is so much like a balloon inflating inside me.

But then it happens, so quietly and indistinctly I hardly notice at first: a tiny, limp hand, flexing and squeezing itself within my own, and a warm trickle of love seeping from Arry's veins into mine. And now there's a picture too, of something long and loose in front of me, so clear I can almost touch it, and I realise it's the cord of love which used to run from Arry's heart to mine, dangling between us like a loose piece of rope – stretched and twisted and split and torn, but still not broken. Trembling, I take hold of one end of the cord and press it to my heart. Then, ever so carefully, I manoeuvre the other end towards Arry's heart and press it in.

Words are pouring out of me. "I love you and forgive you, Arry. I love you and forgive you. Forget the Shaun thing, just come back to me. Please, Arry, come back. I miss you. Mum misses you. Sammy misses you. Dad misses you. Bruno misses you. I LOVE YOU AND FORGIVE YOU, ARRY. I love you, love you, love you. Please, *please*, come back…"

My body's juddering. I can't stay upright. I'm tipping forwards, terrified of falling onto Arry, but I can't stop myself. The sofa's under me. Sammy's nuzzling hard, so hard, and I'm falling, falling, falling…

There's a hand on the base of my neck, cool and light as an angel's. Arry's hand. There's a deep peace encircling me. There's never-ending love. I think someone is coming towards me. It looks like it could be Mum, but I can't be sure because my vision is dimmed, and the face is blurred with tears.

Chapter Sixteen

Ever so gradually, Arry starts to get better, Bruno begins his migration away from the front door, Sammy stops cowering under the kitchen table, and Mum starts smiling again. As for me, well I become Arry's self-appointed guardian angel, watching over her, banishing any stray dark thoughts that creep into her head, and drawing her from those momentary lapses when she seems to be slipping from us again. When I'm not doing all these things, I'm putting up with her droning on about how boring illness is and how she can't wait to get back to normal. In all this time, she doesn't mention Shaun once, and I don't either. What happened belongs to the past, and we both know that.

However, ten days into her convalescence, I'm woken from this beautiful sleep by a blood-curdling scream. I leap from my bed and rush into her.

"We were in this cave," she shrieks "and there were flames licking round you. I was trying to stamp them out, but they were too high, and I had to dive in to rescue you. Behind me, I heard Shaun screaming his head off. He was running through the flames… and… and…"

But she's too upset to tell me the rest, and I'm too upset to listen. I do my best to calm her, before going downstairs to make us both a Horlicks. When I get back, she makes this announcement:

"I'm going to ditch him, Sadie. What I did to you was terrible and I *never, ever* want to hurt you again."

Most probably, Shaun thinks he's been ditched anyway. But it's a brave and selfless thing to promise and, what's more, she means it. She'll give up Shaun for me, and for the sake of the love buoying and steadying us now in the pale red afterglow of her nightmare – even though it will break her heart to do it. And I just can't let her.

"There's no need," I say gently. "You don't have to ditch him for me."

"I do! I do!" she cries.

"You don't! You don't!" I cry back.

"Why not?" she asks.

"Cos I'm over him, Arry. Shaun was definitely just a crush for me, but he's much, much more for you. Anyway, it would probably kill you to do it, and if you don't mind, I'd rather have a rat for a brother-in-law than a corpse for a twin. Just don't expect me to tag along with you guys any more!"

A smile comes to her face then, the first in ages, so full and peaceful it fills my heart with joy.

Come what may, Shaun Wilson's here to stay.

***

I know Arry's back to normal when she won't stop pestering me about who I fancy instead of Shaun. At first, I'm reluctant to say. I mean, it's no joke telling the most boy-crazy girl on the planet your solitary gay secret. But then I think: *What the hell? She's my twin, isn't she, and if I can't tell my twin, who can I tell?*

"You really want to know?"

"Yes!" she exclaims.

"Promise you won't laugh?"

"Promise."

"Well… you remember that German girl Shaun dumped on me – the one I had to look after while you were rehearsing *A Midsummer Night's Dream*?"

"You mean that weird girl I didn't get, and Shaun couldn't wait to see the back of?"

"Yes. Her name is Anneliese, and she isn't weird, just different. Well, she sort of became a friend…"

"And?"

"And I…"

"And you invited her over, up to your bedroom – the sacred

room *no-one* must enter – and started snogging her."

"Yes!" I gasp. "How did you know?"

I expect her to say: "I'm your twin. I know all your thoughts, don't I." But what she actually says is:

"I don't know, do I! I'm *joking*, Sadie. I'm just finishing the story for you; stringing you along, the way you are me. There's about as much chance of you fancying that girl, or any other girl for that matter, as there is of you fancying Faz, i.e. NIL!"

She leans across the breakfast table and clicks her fingers in front of my face, like one of those sexy Spanish dancers. "Come on, be serious, who is *he*?"

"No-one," I say, sliding away into my shell and wishing I'd never come out of it. My twin just doesn't get it: doesn't get that I'm not boy-mad like her; doesn't get my feelings for Anneliese; doesn't get, for one second, that I'm in the middle of this life-changing discovery about myself and what I need most is her understanding and support. She thinks because I'm younger than her by *only* fifteen minutes (and therefore a kind of extension of her), there's no way I could fancy girls instead of boys, and no way I'd rather nuzzle up to Anneliese than Shaun, because there's no way *she* would.

Which leaves me lost for words and backed into a corner and building, building, building inside with all the anguish, desperation and heartache of an inner truth aching to come out. But who can I tell if Arry won't believe me? Mum? Dad? Bruno? Mrs Hodges next door? It's too risky a decision to be left to personal choice, so I decide to deliver it up to fate, write four names on four pieces of paper, shake them around in one of my shoes and pull one out.

And the name that comes out is DAD, which isn't so bad. I mean, it could have been MRS HODGES, in which case I'd have to shake, shake and shake again. But Dad's OK because:

1. I won't have to face him across the breakfast table each morning knowing he knows my secret.

123

2. He's made such a mess of his own relationship, he can't exactly complain about me going off the straight and narrow.
3. He speaks fluent German and can teach me to speak it, so I can get even closer to Anneliese.

When I get to ten Orchard Close, I tell him instantly. He's pretty laid-back about it. I mean, he doesn't exactly fling his arms round me and say it's the best news he's been given since I popped into the world as surprise baby number two. But he doesn't fling me out of his house, either, or withdraw silently and disapprovingly, like some dads might, or sit me down and try to talk me out of my feelings for Anneliese. He just flicks on the kettle, spoons the coffee into the mugs, plucks an apple from the fruit bowl, bites into it and declares in his deepest, most resonant voice ever, "Oranges are not the only fruit, Sadie. There are apples, bananas, lemons, plums, pears and peaches to name but a few; and life's not just black and white, but many shades of grey. Maybe Anneliese is a crush, maybe she isn't. Maybe you love her, maybe you don't. But one thing I know for sure – there's only one way to find out!"

Dad's whole speech is a little bit cryptic and takes a few minutes to work out, but once I have, I feel a whole heap better, like a pressure cooker with its valve yanked out, and with a voice inside my head saying: *Go for it, Sadie! Go! Go! Go!*

This voice doesn't go away – it just gets louder. It pounds in my head when I'm trying to sleep. It nags me when I'm soaking in the bath. It plays havoc with my common sense and my online chat. *GO FOR IT, SADIE! GO! GO! GO!*

I would, only I'm terrified! It's five days, three hours and one minute since *I* kissed Anneliese, and five days, three hours and zero minutes since *she* kissed me back. Chances are she's forgotten our lips ever met. But I can't forget my one and only trip to paradise.

When I lick my lips, I can still taste the lemony sweetness of her skin, shot through with a hint of fiery red chillies. When I undress at night, I imagine her auburn hair unravelling over my body. But I haven't even had the guts to text "hi" to her. To make matters worse, the only time I thought I saw her weaving through the park on her bike, I behaved like an idiot, charged after the bike and almost hurled myself on top of it, only to discover it wasn't Anneliese at all, but some girl who gave me a mouthful. She didn't have Anneliese's beauty, or her warm, kind smile, or that look of light in her eyes which refuses to go away.

So now it's three-thirty on a miserable afternoon in early November, and I'm in our dining room trying to figure out the best way to bump into Anneliese for real. Time's running out. If I don't act soon, she'll be on her way back to Germany and I'll never, ever see her again.

Shaun strolls into our dining room – alone. He and Arabella have kissed and made up in a way which would make Romeo and Juliet look lukewarm, managed to extract a thumbs-up from Mum about their hot new relationship, and now Shaun uses our house like it's his own. At first, he doesn't see me because our dining room is painted dark green and it's hard to make people out in the shadows, but then he spots me, thinks I'm Arabella and very nearly does something too embarrassing for words. Twigs just in time, thank God!

After that, we don't know where to look. It's the first time we've been alone together since his act of treachery, and his instinct is to scuttle off. Only, I call him back. I think he thinks if he hangs around for too long, I'll turn nasty and pelt him with Bruno's miniature ball bearings, or flick salt in his eye from Mum's salt cellar. But I'm past revenge and instead I give him my most enigmatic look *ever*.

"What's up, Sadie?" he asks.

"Nothing," I reply enigmatically. "I just wondered how Anneliese is getting on. I haven't seen her for ages."

He rolls his eyes impatiently.

"Still boring everyone with her moods. I reckon she's hooked on some boy or something, the way she's acting. Not that I really care."

"Oh," I say coolly.

But it's pretty obvious Shaun's in no mood to talk about Anneliese, and if I'm to get any information out of him, I'll have to work quickly and somehow transform him from the human equivalent of a hard, underripe banana into a soft, mushy, overripe one, ready to burst out of its skin.

My enigmatic look evaporates and is replaced by a sickly smile (but not *so* sickly he gets the wrong idea) and I start lavishing compliments on him like there's no tomorrow: how he's the best sax player for miles and could easily win *Young Musician of the Year*; how I've never seen an Oberon like his (though, admittedly, I've only seen one); how he *must* apply to RADA because he's definitely good enough, and he and Arry could go together and be lovers in the same plays, and I'd come and watch every production and laugh the loudest, cry the loudest and clap the loudest. And by the end of my sickly spiel, Shaun *is* an overripe banana, and I could squeeze *anything* out of him!

"So, what do you think is up with Anneliese?" I ask.

"Well, the way her eyes keep changing colour and she moons around the place, she must be in love. Guess what? I caught her writing something the other day, but as soon as I walked in, she hid the piece of paper under the desk and wouldn't say what it was. Next thing I know, she's crying on the stairs like her cat's just died; but as far as I know, there is no cat or dog or guinea pig or goldfish or hamster for that matter, and her folks are just fine. And I thought Arry was mushy in love! God! Sorry, Sadie. I didn't mean to mention Arry and me. Sorry! Sorry! Sorry!"

But I hardly notice Shaun's gaffe, I'm so desperate to hear more.

"But she hasn't actually said she's in love?"

"Nope. Won't say, will she. She flies home on Saturday, so we can all get some peace."

"Saturday? What, *this* Saturday?"

"Yeah. What's so surprising about that? She's been here ages. It's time she went home. You were great with her, Sadie. I owe you."

Pictures storm my head of Anneliese striding towards the plane at Heathrow, her hair bouncing all over the place, her eyes fixed on the pilot who'll whizz her back to Germany and make her forget all about Britain and me, and I have to stifle a gulp.

"She flies at eight in the morning. Dross time, if you ask me. I mean, what kind of flight scheduler makes you get up at four a.m.? Dad was going to take her to the airport, but he's got an early morning meeting, and Mum's busy too, so she has to go on her own in a taxi."

Pictures of Anneliese clambering into a taxi in the dead of night, clutching her rucksack for comfort, while Shaun and his parents wave her off in their dressing gowns. Anneliese: all cold and lonely and frightened, without me to hold her hand.

"Apparently, her mum's not bothered; says Anneliese is used to travelling alone and has friends dotted all over the globe. She just flies from country to country, visiting them all."

Pictures of Anneliese touching base in Istanbul, where an exotic teenage goddess greets her with a kiss, whisks her off to her konak, wraps her in silk and feeds her Turkish delight all afternoon. And me, astray in the cold, cold dark of the park, without Anneliese to hold my hand.

"… and there was this *P.S.* carved in the wood."

"What?" I say, because all the time Shaun's been wittering on, my imagination has been trekking the globe with Anneliese, and I could well have missed something vital.

"I said I found this *P.S.* carved on the desk in Anneliese's room. I've been trying to figure out what it could mean. Maybe she was hacked off and meant to carve *PISS* but didn't have the guts or didn't know how to spell it or didn't have the heart to deface a science professor's desk with slang when we've all been so nice to her, so just wrote *P.S.* instead. Or maybe she was writing a letter, and the *P.S.* came through on the wood. Anyway, there it was, clear as anything: *P.S.* on the desk."

My heart misses a beat. *P.S.* on the desk. Like Shaun says, it could stand for *PISS* or *P.S.* But what if it's nothing to do with rude words or postscripts or anything Shaun thinks it's to do with, but with something more mysterious and private, and the letters have been turned around to keep their meaning secret? What if in Germany when you're in love with someone and want to keep it secret, you switch round the person's initials to disguise them? What if Anneliese has deliberately changed *S.P.* to *P.S.* because she doesn't want the Wilsons to know she's in love with SADIE PREECE – with ME!

"Are you OK, Sadie? You look a bit funny," Shaun says.

"I'm OK," I say, but I'm not OK at all.

"I should never have mentioned the L word, should I? I've upset you. I still like you a lot, Sadie. I'd never want to hurt you. I…"

"Shut up, Shaun!" I shout, putting up my hand to silence him.

If *only* he knew, if *only* he realised, whatever he says, however he says it, he can't hurt me any more. He no longer has the power to affect my feelings because he no longer has a place in my inner world.

"You haven't upset me, Shaun. I'm over you and have been for ages. But there's something mega urgent I have to do. Tell Mum and Arry I've gone out, will you?"

Chapter Seventeen

I race out of the house and nearly get knocked over by a load of cars, my head's so full of Anneliese and getting to her in time. Somehow, I manage to clamber onto the number eleven bus, which will take me to the corner of Lime Tree Avenue.

"Long time no see," the driver mutters morosely. "Not planning a multi-circuit today, then?"

"No. Just a return fare to Lime Tree Avenue, please."

The bus crashes along at high speed, jerks to a halt when I ping the bell and drops me at the café. Ahead of me, houses sparkle like buildings on a marble film set, and at the very end of the avenue sits Treffonen, the star mansion that will make or break my life. I'm so nervous, I don't know how to get myself up the avenue, let alone up the steps to the front door, till I remember Arry's yoga breaths, where you breathe in deeply, push out your stomach and release sharply. Five times I try this, and by my fifth breath I'm at the house, pulling on the cord.

Mrs Wilson appears and observes me cautiously from the top of the marble steps.

"I'm afraid Shaun isn't here, Sadie. He's gone to meet… your twin," and she looks away, really embarrassed.

"Oh, that's OK, Mrs Wilson. It's not Shaun I've come to see. It's Anneliese."

There's this rustling sound inside the house, and a human form skirts the back of the hall, but it's too dark to tell if it's Anneliese or Professor Wilson or even the in-house ghost, making a fleeting daytime appearance.

"Anneliese? Why, she's here. Come on out, dear."

As Anneliese appears in the doorway, I hardly dare look at her in case her beauty overwhelms me. It's impossible not to look at her, though. For one thing, it's what I've been longing to do all week; for another, it's pretty rude to turn up on someone's doorstep and not look at the person you've come to see.

So, I try half looking at her, narrowing and screwing up my eyes and squinting up into the porch at sections of her beauty: the dark, velvet slope of her eyebrows; the cute, triangular scar in the middle of her forehead; the red, heart-shaped tip quivering tantalisingly on her top lip.

"Hi," I murmur.

"Hi," she murmurs back, as frosty white tendrils of her breath curl and coil towards me.

"Er… sorry I didn't come yesterday or the day before," (or the day before that and that, I'm thinking and kicking myself), "only…"

"It does not matter," she says quickly, shooting an awkward glance at Mrs Wilson.

"Why don't you both come into the sitting room, where there's a log fire," Mrs Wilson says. "It's too cold to be chatting out here."

"No thanks, Mrs Wilson!" I practically scream – because the last place I want to be is in *that* sitting room, on *that* chaise longue, where Shaun and I had *that* snog.

Mrs Wilson looks at me, stunned.

"It's just that there's something I *have* to show Anneliese in town… before the shops close."

"Ah, I see," she says, like she really *does* see, right through my naff little excuse. "Do you want to go to town, Anneliese?"

"Sure. I will just get my jacket."

But if Mrs Wilson does suspect, she's too nice to ask questions, and definitely too nice to go gossiping to neighbours about how Sadie Preece used to go out with her son, but now she's nuts about this German girl instead. She just scans the skyline, murmurs something about snow coming from the north and wafts away, leaving Anneliese and me alone on the steps.

Course I want to be alone with Anneliese – it's what I've been trying to negotiate for the last ten minutes, so I *definitely* won't be walking off. But it's still not easy being face to face with *the* sexiest girl on earth and having nobody and nothing to hide behind (not even my squint, which is fading fast). My head's like an empty bucket, with all the impressive things I had stored in it deposited down someone's drain.

If Anneliese feels anything like me, she's certainly not showing it. Glistening with cool, misty autumn beauty, she glides down the steps, rests her hand gently on my shoulder, flips over, adjusts the flap on her trainer and scoops herself up – all in the space of an ultra-sophisticated ten seconds, while strands of her red, flaming hair tickle my kneecaps, and lemony bursts from her skin zoom up my nostrils, and I very nearly keel over with desire for her.

"Zo, Sadie, this thing you want to show me in the shops – can I take it home?"

"Er, no, not exactly," I say.

We start walking then, which helps a bit because it gives me something other than Anneliese to think about, i.e. where to put each foot.

"But if I like it, it is possible you will buy it for me, and I will enjoy it here?"

"Well, I could do; only, it's not really like that, Anneliese. I mean, if I were rich, course I'd buy you lots of things, but I'm not and I don't have any spare money on me… and the actual *thing* you're talking about… well… actually, it doesn't really exist. It never did. I just made it up to get you to…"

My words trail away like dead leaves through the winter sky. What does it matter what I meant to get her to do? She'd never agree to it anyway. It would never work. What happened in my bedroom was a mistake. Coming here today was a mistake. Right now, being me feels like a mistake.

"To what?" she says, stopping dead in the middle of the pavement as the traffic thunders past us. "What were you going to get me to do, Sadie?"

"Nothing," I say.

"Please, Sadie. I really want to know."

"It's nothing; just this stupid idea I got stuck in my head that... er... after what happened that time... up in my bedroom... you liked me... more than a friend, and if I could summon the guts, I'd ask you to this place on the edge of town where we'd hang out before you go back to Germany. But it won't happen, so it doesn't matter."

It's not my greatest speech. Shakespeare wouldn't be impressed, and it certainly wouldn't make *me* hang out with someone. But Anneliese is looking at me deadly seriously.

"Zo, this *thing* you were telling Mrs Wilson about is not a thing but a place?"

"Yes," I say.

"And it is not in town but on the edge of town, away from people?"

"Sort of."

"And you would like us to go there – just you and me?"

"Well, that was the idea," I say.

Suddenly, the look of light, which until this moment has remained dormant beneath a dark shadow of disguise, bursts onto Anneliese's face.

"Come here, Sadie," she murmurs.

Nearly blinded by her light, I step towards her on the pavement. She places her hands around my ear, presses her smooth, silky lips to my icy earlobe and whispers: "Of course I don't want to go shopping. I want to be on my own with you, Sadie."

No-one's told me what to do when you discover that the girl you think doesn't fancy you one bit, fancies you like mad after all! I'm a gibbering wreck and just stand there, gibbering.

"Bu... bu... but... I didn't think you liked me. You... you... ran off. You didn't phone or text. I thought I'd made a MASSIVE mistake!"

"Well, you were wrong, weren't you," she says quietly.

She's stroking my hair now; catching stray strands that have been tossed by the wind and sweeping them gently behind my ears. It's a mixed-up sensation of part bliss and part terror, as I relish her touch on the softest, most sensitive part of my ear, while frantically keeping my eyes pinned to the passing cars.

"I've always fancied you, Sadie."

"*Have you? Really?*"

"Yes. *Really!*"

"What, even when I was wearing that yucky green cagoule and those flat, brown lace-ups, and looked the opposite of young, cool and hip?"

"Yes! Anyway, it's not what you wear, it's the way that you wear it. You could wear an astronaut suit and look good in it, because you have your own special brand of Sadie style. I was dead jealous of Shaun, but I could hardly tell you when you were going out with him, and I only ran off from your bedroom that time because… I was scared. Dead scared, Sadie."

"*Scared?* Of what? You must have kissed *loads* of girls. You must have *loads* of experience!"

"Who says?"

"Well, no-one, exactly. I just think you must because you're so mature and sexy and…"

"No," she says, shaking her head violently. "It is not like that at all. Perhaps one or two girls have been interested, but most do not want to know. They run a mile, or they do it for a laugh and a dare, and you end up feeling used and rejected, just searching for that special someone."

"I'm sorry," I say. "It must be really tough."

"It does not matter. Just give me a hug and I will feel better."

"A hug? What, here?"

"Yes, here!"

"On the street?"

"I am only asking for a hug, Sadie. I am not asking you to strip off."

"OK," I say, and I try to relax and let my arms loosen and open, but they just flip out like Dalek arms, and I end up giving Anneliese the stiffest, most robotic hug this planet has ever witnessed.

"Relax," she whispers in my ear. "Look, this is how you hug someone you fancy," and her arms loop around my body. Her lips brush over my cheeks, depositing cool, wintry puffs of breath on my skin. Her lips skate towards my lips and we *very* nearly kiss. She holds me close for several seconds.

"Come on, let's go to this place," she says, linking her arm through mine and keeping it there all the way to the park.

I feel less like a robot in the park. It's easier to relax here because it's dusk and there are no cars and virtually no staring people – just a handful of joggers crossing the wide, open spaces like moving icicles, and they're not remotely interested in Anneliese and me.

"Zo, Sadie, this is the place?" Anneliese says, looking around and shivering.

"Yes. Sorry it's not indoors. I did think of taking you to the Odeon or Pizza Palace or even the multi-storey car park, but none of those places are as private as the park."

"No problem," she says, her teeth clicking like cicadas and a quirky smile breaking through them. "So long as you don't mind freezing to death, Sadie!"

Then I remember the arboretum, where, in the month of June, birds sing, sap oozes, small animals procreate, blossoms burst forth, and willows and birches cascade lattice-like over people's heads, like marriage bowers; and where, in November, the steady plop of water from the trees, the dark, hidden spaces, enclosed by shadows and fir trees and fortressed by piles of dead leaves, make it the most private place I can think of and, with any luck, two degrees warmer. We weave around the back of the empty bandstand, along by the children's play area, in and out of the rhododendron bushes, and up the steep bank to the heart of the arboretum.

"It should be a bit warmer in here," I say, trying to sound positive.

"Zo," Anneliese says.

"Zo… zo," I stammer, because I know damn well that now we're here she's waiting for me to make the next move. Then the stupidest, most embarrassing thing happens – I get a mammoth dose of hiccups! They come from nowhere: these loud, repulsive cupping sounds, hopping and popping from my mouth every time I try to speak, and I'm cursing that Golden Delicious apple I had at lunchtime cos Anneliese will *never* fancy me now.

How wrong I am.

"You're *zo* funny, Sadie," she giggles, leaning back against this giant spruce and watching my hiccups hop and pop from my mouth. "That's why I fancy you zo *very, very* much."

She stretches her arms above her head and stares at me mesmerically. She looks incredible up against that tree, all moulded with the mossy twists and turns of the bark, her breasts jutting hauntingly from beneath her jacket, her eyes on me, deep and dark as midnight. So incredible, my hiccups stop. I think of all the things I could do then, like French kiss her, or nibble her earlobe, or try to get under her clothes to her naked skin, but she's wearing a brown woolly jacket, and a jumper and a shirt, and maybe a vest and a bra under them, and it could amount to a full-scale expedition!

Anyway, I'm terrified she'll run off. So, when she shivers next, I just unzip her jacket, edge a little closer, slide my arms inside and hook my fingers in the loops of her belt, letting them hang there. She giggles a bit more, and I'm not sure if this is because of my hiccups or if she's embarrassed we're suddenly *this* close, but then she starts making all these little nuzzling sounds and nuzzles closer, so I can feel her breasts taut against mine, and her face cold and damp from the air, and her hair loaded with droplets of rain water, and when I look into her eyes again, there's that luminous look of light.

Then I'm opening the top three buttons of her shirt, pressing down the material so that it makes a V shape against her skin, stroking my little finger over her firm, dark goose bumps and searching for that beautiful brown mole I couldn't take my eyes off once – the one which lies just beneath her collarbone. She's trembling; I'm trembling. I'm pressing my lips to her mole and spreading my whole tongue over it. I'm pulling down her shirt some more, tracing my fingers over her silky breast, searching for that other magic point and finding it – cold and hard and tight as a frost-encased woodland berry, which warms and softens under my tongue.

Then my tongue is travelling up her neck, slinking towards her mouth. My hand is sliding between her thighs, finding the opening in her jeans, inching beneath the denim, touching, fingering the soft swell inside, and my tongue is feeling its way around the warm enclosure of her mouth. And it's heaven.

I stop and together we release a little sigh.

"Do it again," she says, and so I do, and by the time we stop a second time I feel about three years older. Anneliese is short of breath, and so am I. She leans back against the tree, presses the hollow of her back into its bark and closes her eyes. I can't stop touching her, she's so incredible.

"What you do to me is amazing, Sadie. *You're* amazing!"

"Am I?" I reply, because for all that we can't keep our hands off each other, this idea is pretty hard to swallow.

"Yes, you are! Do me a favour – when you get home tonight, take a long, long look in the mirror and try to see the *amazing, beautiful* Sadie I see."

I drop back my head. Above, the sky is a pool of deep orange. Anneliese's fingers are running all over me, like streams of coloured light.

"*Try,*" she murmurs.

"I'll try," I murmur, and then we're kissing like we'll never stop.

I don't know what time it is when we come out of the arboretum. All I know is it's a whole lot darker, and I'm not the same Sadie as went in. I'm not even the Sadie I was after Shaun and Arabella did what they did and my whole world fell apart. I'm different from the last Sadie and the Sadie before that. For one thing, I doubt I'll ever have hiccups like those again, i.e. mammoth ones, which represent a life-altering moment. For another, I know now what French kissing *really* is, and it's definitely *not* going round and round on the same old bus. For a third thing, I'm totally in love.

Really in love. Not like with Shaun, where I thought I was in love but wasn't. *Really, truly in love.* I have to be, otherwise why do I get dizzy whenever Anneliese comes near, and why does the thought of losing her gut me so much I could even cry in front of the neighbours; and while we're on the neighbours, why am I suddenly thinking really nice things about Mrs Hodges, when most of the time I think she's a nosy old crow?

This is no illusion of love. It's for real, and because it's for real it's going to take more than a couple of Mum's antacids to get my stomach back to the calm, functioning organ it was before I met Anneliese, and more than an average dose of willpower to put aside my dizzy feelings, re-summon sensible Sadie and focus on getting the two of us out of this park before the night completely sets in.

Focusing isn't easy, not least because when you've been snuggled up with your lover in a green, mossy space, with only a squirrel and a few blackbirds for company, getting back into the real world comes as a bit of a shock. As Anneliese and I grope our way towards the bandstand, the world swaggers and sways before our eyes like a twilight-stricken drunk, its huge, darkened shapes reeling towards us, its piercing headlights pouncing from the roadside, its yells and hollers drumming through our ears.

"I don't want you to go," Anneliese cries.

"I don't want to go, either," I cry back.

I hold her close under the rusting canopy of the Victorian bandstand, where lovers have met for over a hundred years, wishing it didn't have to be like this: that we never had to say goodbye, or that love wasn't this strangely mixed-up thing where you feel sky-high one minute and rock-bottom the next.

"It won't be forever," I say.

She nods, like she believes me, but I can tell she's really unhappy, and her pain traverses every cell in my body.

"I'll text every day, Anneliese, and tell my folks about us, and fly to Munich to see you. And I'll learn German faster than you can say *sprechen sie Deutsch*!"

The look of light skims her tear-stained face, like a ray of moonlight skimming water, and I wonder how long it will be before we're together again. We pull away from each other, as the cold night air severs us like a wedge.

"Why does saying goodbye have to hurt zo very, very much, Sadie?"

"I don't know," I say, because at the end of the day, I just don't. Even if I read every love poem ever written, I still couldn't explain why saying goodbye to someone I've known less than four months should hurt *this* much. So much, my heart is splitting.

"I'll see you, Anneliese," I say.

"See you," she cries, and we turn and go our separate ways.

***

That night, I do look in the mirror. I can't say I see exactly what Anneliese sees, i.e. someone *amazing* and *beautiful*. I mean, when you've never seen yourself as *amazing* and *beautiful* and someone suddenly asks you to do just that, it's a bit like being asked to believe the most far-fetched story in the Bible when you've never really believed in God. But I'm working on it, and even though I don't get the full story, I've started to notice something amazing about my eyes, which has never really struck me before.

I'm starting to understand something about love, too – that maybe love is when someone sees something special in you that you can't see yourself until love shows you the way, and then you start to believe it.

Chapter Eighteen

My heart lifts and dips a second time that week when I arrive home to see Mum looking more beautiful than she's looked in years, framing the open doorway like a dreamy maiden, her golden highlights cascading around her shoulders, one of those floaty Per Una dresses coiled around her hourglass figure, and her eyes pinned to Dad (of all people), easing himself out of his Golf.

Don't get me wrong – not for one second do I think this is the prelude to some kind of reconciliation between my parents. I long gave up hoping and wishing and praying they'd get back together. But that said, I'd have to be pretty switched off not to spot there's some serious chemistry going on here. Mum can't take her eyes off Dad, Dad can't take his eyes off Mum, and Bruno, wherever he is, might as well have flown to Mars!

There are certain times when it's best not to gate-crash your parents' private stuff; when it's far wiser to hover tactfully on the periphery of the action rather than smash right into it, and this is *definitely* one of them. My parents haven't seen each other for a good year, and it shows – it *really, really* shows! The air throbs and bristles with all the pent-up energy of their nights spent apart; with all the regret and longing of long-lost dreams, all the tension of things said and not said, and with all the hopes, urges, grudges and hang-ups of them both.

And *because* they haven't seen each other for so long, this is high voltage stuff, condensed like unexploded gunpowder into just ninety seconds. There's the hypnotic way they look each other up and down, up and down, oblivious of everyone and everything around them; there's the ooze and slime of all Dad's guilt, breaking out like a ginormous overripe spot as he squirms and writhes on

139

the tarmac and casts mournful glances of regret up at their old bedroom window and down at Mum, and then there's all Mum's anger and sadness bubbling away.

Then there's me, right on the edge of it all (except when are you really *ever* on the edge of your parents' stuff?), wondering *what* my dad is up to, *what* he's playing at, *what*, in fact, he's doing here *at all!* Doesn't he realise this is *no-go* territory, and Mum's feelings *no-go* with it? He can't just turn up here, play her like some slot machine, whack her feelings round some great metal maze and expect them to fall into his lap like a load of one-pound coins. Obviously, he *doesn't* get this because instead of doing the decent thing and retreating quietly, he's doing the opposite! He's harnessing himself for action. He's tossing sense and caution to the wind. He's mounting his great white charger and he's heading towards Mum and is about to cry, "You look *absolutely gggggg...*," and he's stopping short of "*orgeous*" and saying:

"You look well, Danielle."

And Mum's saying: "Do I?"

And Dad's saying: "Yes... *incredibly* well!"

And before we know it, we're back in that dreamy, hypnotic space, where they can't take their eyes off each other and where no-one else exists, and this really could be the prelude to a kiss and *would* be, if Bruno didn't suddenly appear in the doorway with a cabbage in one hand and a vegetable knife in the other, and Mum didn't swiftly flick a roving tear from her cheek and smile up at him, and Dad didn't take the biggest step back I have ever seen anyone take in a suburban drive the size of a postage stamp.

It's the first time Dad and Bruno have *ever* set eyes on each other, and if first impressions are anything to go by, most likely the last, too.

Looking *really* tense, Bruno says: "You must be Justin," and jams the vegetable knife hard into the cabbage to free up his right hand.

Looking just as tense, Dad says: "You must be Bruno," and extends a quivering hand to him.

Then no-one knows what to say, and so I come out of the garage, where I've been lurking for the last five minutes, and everyone stares at me like I'm some kind of alien – which I suppose is normal in a situation fit for aliens.

"Hi Mum. Hi Dad. Hi Bruno," I say, sloping towards (and with any luck past) them.

"Why, Sadie, how long have you been out here?" Dad asks, stunned by my sudden appearance.

"Not long," I say and shoot upstairs to Arry's room, because the tension's just too much to take any more.

"*What the hell is going on?*" I scream. "*Dad's outside with Bruno!*"

"I know," Arry yawns, like it's the most natural thing in the world for Dad and Bruno to get together. "He's come for dinner."

"*What?*"

"While you were out, he phoned up, invited himself to dinner and made *me* the excuse – some rubbish about needing to re-bond with me on my own territory because I'm putting out this message of being emotionally and psychologically alienated by his new house. In other words, he's pissed off I never visit him, so he's turned up here. *He* thinks it's a really smart idea. *I* say it's his worst to date."

"He must be mad! Doesn't he know how jealous Bruno gets?" I say, frantically demisting Arry's bedroom window to check Dad isn't hurtling across the front garden on the end of Bruno's fist.

"Why would he? You know how stubborn he is, Sadie. Once he's set his mind on something, there's no stopping him. You better start praying fast!"

When Arry and I go down five minutes later (Arry first, me following), Mum, Dad and Bruno are huddled together in the hall. This I don't get. I mean, you're in this tricky, potentially explosive situation, where two of you secretly hate each other's guts but are trying not to, the third person is the reason you hate each other's guts but are trying not to, and you all decide to squash up in the darkest, stuffiest, most claustrophobic part of the house, where any second all manner of emotions could let rip, when you could be in a large, airy sitting room, with plenty of space to set your boundaries and plenty of fresh air circulating to diffuse the tricky atmosphere. I mean, you wouldn't do it, would you, unless you were spoiling for a fight?

Anyway, they're all huddled in the hall, and if Arry finds it hard to face Dad after two years of not seeing him, she certainly covers it up well, taking the stairs with the sublime assurance of a supermodel on the catwalk.

Dad turns to look up at her. It's a breathtakingly beautiful moment, which I can't help thinking would make an exquisite painting or photograph: two pairs of the same cornflower blue eyes, connecting for the first time in years; tipping and spilling around their edges to form a limpid, liquid blue reflection of each other, a pure distillation of love and emotion.

"Hi Dad," Arabella murmurs, pausing momentarily on the middle stair.

"Arabella," Dad stammers, "I can't believe it! You've grown so much. I hardly recognise you! Goodness, Danielle, hasn't she grown? You're practically a young woman. You're absolutely beautiful!"

Dad's running his hands through his hair in disbelief, turning to Mum, to me, to Bruno, even to the empty corners of the hall for any assurance he can get that this vision before him really *is* his daughter.

We're all looking at Arry now, each one of us noticing the person she's become – not like Dad in a huge leap of a way, but with the gradual registering of everyday contact – a softer, lovelier, Alex-free version of her old self. Like Dad, I feel her wonder.

"Thanks for coming," Arabella says quietly.

"How could I not?" Dad exclaims. "It's been two years, Arry. Two long, gruelling years without you. Way too long to be away from my baby. We must *never* let it go this long again. We must try… we must so try to…"

And suddenly Arry's chucking off her model pose and tearing down the stairs. Her necklace is lassoing her, her hair's flying everywhere, her arms are flailing wildly, and she's flinging herself into Dad's arms.

"My darling, my darling," Dad's shouting, as he clutches and kisses her. "My darling, my darling, my darling…"

"Dad… Dad… Dad!" Arry's sobbing.

I hardly dare look at Mum. Tears are plunging down her face. I'm forcing my hands through the narrow wooden slats in the bannisters, trying to reach her. The wood's ripping my skin, creating tiny white rucks of broken flesh along the insides of my arms, but I've found Mum's hands and I'm rubbing them hard, and she's crying and rubbing mine back. Dad and Arry are clinging to each other like nothing will *ever* part them. Then Dad's turning his grief-stricken face to Mum, stretching out his arm to her and drawing her into their hug, and Mum's going there, *all the way*, pulling me with her so hard my shoulder cracks and my face jams against the points in the bannisters, and I can hardly take it – all this love and all this agony. Sixty whole seconds of it – of being the family we used to be again.

Then the hug's over and Arry's letting go of Dad, Dad's letting go of Mum, Mum's letting go of me and I'm letting go of the bannisters and rubbing my shoulder and my sore nose and looking round for Bruno – who is absolutely nowhere to be seen.

My instant thought is to go search for him, and so when the others troop into the sitting room, I do a quick detour via the kitchen. I spot him over by the cooker, trailing a spoon through the steaming saucepan and staring pensively into the potatoes. I'm relieved to say he doesn't look *too* upset – just kind of distant, as though a part of him has gone off on a journey of its own, miles from our house and our family. I don't like to ask what journey or where or if I can join him on it, so I just wait here, hoping the missing part will come back soon.

"Cheer up, kid. It may never happen," he suddenly says, turning and noticing me.

"I just came to check you're OK."

"I'm OK, but the potatoes aren't! They've turned to mush," he says and then adds ever so seriously, "and it seemed like you needed some family time together, so I made myself scarce."

He puts down his spoon, comes over to me and, placing a reassuring arm around my bruised shoulder, steers me into the sitting room. For a while, then, things go amazingly smoothly, and it even seems as though Dad and Bruno could be friends – till Sammy crops up. Not for real, of course, because he's been banished to the back garden, but in Dad's chitchat.

"Where's Sammy?" Dad asks.

"He's outside in his kennel," Bruno replies, a bit too smugly for comfort.

"In his *kennel*?" Dad exclaims, horrified.

Arry and I exchange a look of "Oh, no" and dip our heads to our chests, while on the sofa Mum stiffens, and Bruno's hand sneaks inside the top of her dress.

"Yep, in his kennel where he belongs," Bruno says.

Poor Dad! How is he supposed to feel with Bruno's hand twitching inside Mum's dress, and the picture of gorgeous little Sammy, a cute little puppy, taunting him with its loveliness from the top of his old desk?

"What's he doing in a kennel? He sleeps in the kitchen, doesn't he?"

"He's a dog, Justin. Dogs sleep in kennels, especially ones as big and boisterous as Sammy. Let him within an inch of the house and everything goes haywire. You can't be too careful with Golden Retrievers, you know!"

"So, he *never, ever* comes into the house?" Dad says.

"Never say never," Bruno quips (*but this is no time for one of Bruno's 007 jokes*). "He comes in occasionally, usually when the girls want him around."

144

Something happens in Dad's head then – something big and wild and dramatic. I don't know if it's because of all the gin he's been knocking back, or news of Sammy, the canine prisoner, or the sudden sight of Bruno's hand jigging around in Mum's dress, or a combination of all three things. One thing's for sure, though – he is *not* a happy man.

He slams down his drink, storms into the kitchen, forces open the back door, storms up to Sammy's kennel, flings it open and stands astride it – proud, defiant, warlike – like an animal rights activist releasing a load of laboratory animals into the wild. Then he grabs hold of Sammy's collar, yanks him into the house and lets him loose on the sitting room, where Sammy, overjoyed to see him, goes absolutely bananas.

"This dog belongs in this house, Bruno, because this is MY DOG, MY HOUSE, THESE ARE MY CHILDREN, AND THIS…" he bellows, pointing a trembling finger at Mum, "IS MY WIFE!"

Hand on heart, this is the only time in sixteen years of existence I've wanted to be Mrs Hodges next door, with no family, no friends and no pets. I wish the earth would swallow me up.

"*Was* your dog, Justin," Bruno mutters gravely from the sofa. "*Was* your house until you decided to vacate it and hand it over to Danielle. *Was* your wife until you signed the divorce papers… shortly to be *my* wife on the twenty-third of September next year."

Dad stares at Bruno utterly gobsmacked. Of course, news of the wedding is old news, even to him, but he still looks like a man who's been told the world's about to end. Then he does the most cringeworthy thing imaginable and starts backtracking on everything he's said and then backtracking on his backtracking, till I'm almost grinding myself into the floor.

"Well, all right, so Sammy isn't my dog any more, but he still thinks I'm his master, you know. Just look at the fuss he's making of me! And legally this may not be my house any more, but I still have a ten per cent stake in it, you know, and Danielle *was* my wife and is shortly to be your wife, but when does the heart ever really change its allegiance, Bruno?"

And the only thing Dad can't backtrack on is the fact that Arry and I are his twins, so he bangs on and on about this, making the whole thing a billion times worse.

I have to hand it to Bruno – he acts like a star. Not once does he rise to Dad's bait, raise his voice or lose his cool. Not once does he try to make Dad look stupid (Dad's managed that perfectly well on his own). He just lays out the facts, one by one, over and over, like he's laying out the same deck of cards, until in the end Dad *has* to back down; which earns Bruno my total respect, and just earns Dad my pity – oodles of it – because however much he might say he wants his freedom and his space and his nice new house, he's obviously gutted about losing us, misses us like crazy and wishes he were living back here again.

Bruno's kindness doesn't stop there, either. Instead of kicking Dad out of the house, he lets him stay for supper. Somehow, we manage to get through it, and by the time Arry and I wave Dad off at nine p.m. things have gone from being really bad to just plain sad.

"I kidded myself tonight would be easy, girls," Dad says. "But from the moment I saw your mother looking stunning on the doorstep, I knew I was in for a tough time. Maybe it's not such a good idea for me to come here in future. Probably best if you come to my place, don't you think?"

We nod in unison (who *wouldn't* after tonight's fiasco) and that's how the new arrangement gets going, with Arry and me going to Dad's every other weekend and treating his nice new house like home.

***

It's late, I'm wrapped in my duvet, and I reckon a new world record has just been set, because there are no sex sounds from Bruno, there's no snoring from Bruno, and there's no noise of any kind from anywhere. There's no message on my mobile from Anneliese either, though I've checked all night for one.

Lying alone, I stare into the darkness. Where the shadow of my wardrobe meets the shadow of the windowpane, *Nu de Dos* is folded in sleep. I watch her slipping into the shadows, till she's submerged by an inky black mass and has gone from me for the night.

Anneliese has gone too, miles and miles from me – across London, through the air, leaving a desolate North Sea churning between us. I miss her so much I nearly board the midnight plane to Munich. Then I nearly bombard her with all these soppy texts that sound like something straight out of the *Shaun and Arry Love Manual,* and only just hit the delete key in time.

In the end, I just lie here, waiting. I'm not sure what I'm waiting for – for things to settle, I suppose. For her life to start up again, and mine too, and for it to sink in that this isn't some stupid crush we'll be over in a week. It's serious. And to pluck up the courage to start telling people this bit of my story: that I thought I loved this English boy but turned out to love this German girl instead.

If I know my family, when I tell them, Dad will be his usual laid-back self, and Mum will be laid-back cos there won't be any pregnancy scares, and Arry (when she *finally* gets round to believing me) will think it's the coolest thing on earth, and Bruno – well, I think I can probably count on Bruno's support. And the only person who won't be laid-back is Great Aunt Eva, who'll huff and puff and try to blast right through all my love for Anneliese. But how much does that really matter, and how often do I see Great Aunt Eva anyway?

And the world at large will be like Janus on his throne: sometimes it will look back to winter and send a cold, sharp wind slicing through me, which will make me want to hide away all my feelings for Anneliese, and sometimes it will look forward to spring and send a warm, balmy breeze, which will draw me out and make my love for her flourish and grow.

Either way, though, I won't have to squeeze into any of my twin's cast-offs any more.

I won't have to suck up to any of her boyfriends.

I won't be Babes.

I won't be Sad.

I'll be someone quite new.

www.ingramcontent.com/pod-product-compliance
Lightning Source LLC
Chambersburg PA
CBHW020137180626
46810CB00004B/1603